ACKNOWLEDGMENTS

Thank you computer for not crashing during this project. Even though we still had some issues, you hung in there for me.

Thank you, Internet, for your vast supply of information. You are mankind's greatest friend.

Thank you Mary C. Simmons for a wonderful cover design that inspired this second edition.

Thank you Kerry Geneva of Writers Resource, Inc. for the editing. You insights were invaluable.

Most of all, thanks to my lovely wife, Karen, for enduring another book. Sometimes the writer's bug can last for days, leaving me in a trance that causes me to delay or skip chores, honey-do's, bill payments, hygiene, meals, and even some favorite TV shows.

Hopefully I will be able to reward her with a nice vacation cruise in the Caribbean. Only we'd best stay clear of the Bermuda Triangle.

Preview

Howdy. Come on in and make yourself at home. Can I get you something to drink?

I have invited you here to tell you an intriguing story. But before we get started, you might want to visit the restroom, because I guarantee once I start, you won't want me to stop.

Here is an excerpt to wet your appetite:

> "Radioman Hay, report to the radio room on the double," I heard over the ship's intercom.
>
> I had the Con (duty) that night and had just taken a break. I could feel the excitement in the radio room as soon as I stepped through the door.
>
> "We just received an S.O.S.," shouted the excited radioman who had been monitoring the emergency band.
>
> A ship was in danger. It turned out to be a Russian trawler. American fleets were always shadowed by these suspicious fishing boats. They were constantly

snooping and spying on U.S. fleets. We knew who they were and what they were doing, and they knew we knew. It was a cat and mouse game, but we couldn't do anything about it in international waters.

International law required us to respond to an S.O.S., so we took advantage of the opportunity to board their vessel. No U.S. personnel had had that opportunity in the past, so our boarding party was very excited to be able to board a Russian spy boat. Everyone's adrenaline was flowing faster than a class five whitewater rapid.

It definitely wasn't a fishing vessel, as we had suspected all along, even though everything about it looked fishy. We couldn't find one fish onboard, let alone a fishing pole. There was however, a lot of fishy electronic equipment, enough that we wondered how the boat could stay afloat.

The Russian crew was completely disoriented. They appeared to be in shock and looked scared shitless. Only one of them spoke. He babbled in broken English, about some strange-looking flying machine, with small hairless creatures hitting them with a beaming light and a crewman gone missing. Nothing he said was making any sense to anyone in our boarding party, except maybe me. I suspected I might know what they had experienced. Something in the back of my mind told me I had been there and done that. However, I felt it best to keep my mouth shut.

We could smell Vodka on their breath, so it was assumed that they had to be drunk. What happened to the ship and its crew was later classified top secret, so if I were to tell you the rest of this story, I'd have to kill you. That might not be good for future book sales. I can say it was another one of those big government cover-ups that you don't hear or read about in the news.

This incident enforced my thoughts that human beings weren't the only living creatures in the universe after all. But my thoughts didn't last long as we were thrown into a war.

An Abduction Revelation

THE COMEBACK KID RETURNS

Revised Edition

THOMAS L. HAY

BALBOA.
PRESS

A DIVISION OF HAY HOUSE

Balboa Press books may be ordered through booksellers or by contacting:

Balboa Press
A Division of Hay House
1663 Liberty Drive
Bloomington, IN 47403
www.balboapress.com
1-(877) 407-4847

ISBN: 978-1-4525-5957-5 (sc)
ISBN: 978-1-4525-5955-1 (hc)
ISBN: 978-1-4525-5956-8 (e)

Library of Congress Control Number: 2012917867

Print information available on the last page.

Balboa Press rev. date: 11/23/2015

TABLE OF CONTENTS

Introduction . . . . *xiii*

CHAPTER ONE *1*
    The Bequest

CHAPTER TWO *13*
    The Inauguration

CHAPTER THREE *35*
    The Transformation

CHAPTER FOUR *55*
    The Conundrum

CHAPTER FIVE *67*
    The Bewilderment

CHAPTER SIX *95*
    The Awakening

CHAPTER SEVEN *105*
    The Phenomenon

CHAPTER EIGHT *113*
    The Inscrutable

CHAPTER NINE *119*
    The Revelation

CHAPTER TEN *127*
    The Journey

CHAPTER ELEVEN 135
    The Dreams
CHAPTER TWELVE 139
    The Supplementary
CHAPTER THIRTEEN 145
    The Besieged
CHAPTER FOURTEEN 155
    The Reconciliation
CHAPTER FIFTEEN 165
    The Surrogate

Epilogue 169
Idioms 171
Song Appendix 185
Author Autobiography 187
Editor Review 189

INTRODUCTION

Welcome To My World

Won't you come on in? Miracles, I guess, still happen now and then. Step into my heart. —Eddie Arnold

Hey, the Kid is back…But then you didn't really know that I had been gone in the first place, did you? Not yet anyway. Wait till you hear what I have to say upon discovering the revelation that sparked this revised edition to my memoirs.

To refresh your memory, following my retirement, I wrote and published my memoirs, *The Comeback Kid.* The project was an invigorating whirlwind of self-enlightenment and an intense emotional journey. It left me wondering who the old fart is that stares back at me from the mirror.

After publishing my memoirs, it occurred to me that I might have some intriguing and mysterious phenomena buried within my subconscious. I began once again to contemplate what had actually happened that night in my youth when I lost control of the car on the deserted country road outside Clinton, Missouri. Was it a freak accident, or according to the evidence, was I abducted?

Did aliens actually abduct my first wife Claudia and me? She has claimed that this happened not once, but twice: once as we were on our way to the courthouse to get married, and the second time while we were on our belated honeymoon. At the time, however, neither of us were aware that it had happened.

The abductions were revealed to her after we separated and divorced. She said she had to divorce me because her spirit persuaded her to become a vegetarian, fast and abstain from sexual activity. This eventually melted the memory blocks implanted by the aliens, unveiled her subconscious, and exposed traumatic and terrifying past experiences.

However, at the time she first told me about this, I didn't believe her. Would you? I just assumed she had a fertile imagination. I was more interested to recover from the heartbreaking divorce she enforced upon me.

But, upon publishing my memoirs, I got to thinking, "What if Claudia was right? What if what she was saying was true?"

Curiosity got the best of this old tomcat. The thought tormented me to no end. I felt that I needed to investigate the possibility that I might have blocked memories buried in my subconscious.

Since age had diminished my sex drive and I could stand to lose a few pounds, I decided to give it a shot. If Claudia was right and I had implanted memory blocks, the way that I could melt them, according to her, would be to follow in her footsteps and adopt her ascetic lifestyle.

OH-MY-GOD! You're not going to believe this, but I discovered she was right! Never in a million years would I have imagined what lay hidden in my subconscious. The memory block melt was agonizing, but fruitful. However, Claudia was only partially right. Naively, she had only seen the tip of the iceberg. I discovered a revelation that exposed the Antarctic.

The revelation was glaringly productive, uncovering peculiar, bizarre dreams that occurred in my sleep. Dreams that were actually memories, of two people who were alike, but existed in separate entities, yet experienced similar life events.

When looking into the mirror, I could recognize the person who stared back, but I didn't know him.

Now, how could that be?

At the time I had no idea.

This dilemma created an identity crisis, disorientation, and some peculiar interpretations. Parallel worlds were tangled in the same dimension. Reality and imagination intermingle, mystifying and tormenting my existence?

Which was real? Maybe both, but then again, maybe neither. To say the least, it was a confusing and complicated relationship.

It became obvious that I had to rewrite my memoirs. A whole new realm of events unearthed hidden revelations that created a complete new life history. Life events that the Kid never knew existed.

If you have read my original memoir, then bear with me. In this revised story, I have repeated some events, to refresh your memory. These events, plus the new developments, stand alone, in its own story. I have added some colorful insights you might find intriguing.

So, how in the world do I share these hidden memories without coming across as an alien abductee prankster? I have concluded that there really is no other way than to just go ahead and spill the beans. You may wonder, is my story reality or fiction? Or maybe a dream? A hallucination, or the product of a fertile imagination gone wild? If this were the case, where did the imaginations come from? Could they have been blocked memories implanted in my subconscious?

It is not my intention to convince you one way or the other. However, you might want to keep in mind the words of Albert Einstein:

The most beautiful thing we can experience is the mysterious. It is the source of all true art and science. He to whom this emotion is a stranger, who can no longer pause to wonder and stand in awe, is as good as dead; his eyes are closed and he is a stranger unto himself.

Life is but a series of events, much like an assorted box of chocolates, and we never know what might come next. I have used songs to introduce and portray my life events. Often when we hear a song, it reminds us of a person, a place, or a time in our lives.

So, here's my story and, yes, I'm sticking to it. But be warned. What I am about to reveal may cause a disturbance in your comfort zone. The world that you think you know may not exist. You are about to embark on one heck of a roller coaster ride. You might want to check that your seat belt is on. For sure, hold onto your hat. Your secured little world is about to be turned upside down and inside out.

Que sera sera, whatever will be, will be. The future might not be what it's cracked up to be and not ours to see—or is it?

Who are the abductors? Where do they come from? Where are they hiding? Do they even exist?

The Comeback Kid returns with stunning revelations that will startle and torment your reality.

CHAPTER ONE

THE BEQUEST

COUNTRY ROAD

And drivin' down the road I get the feelin'
that I should have been home yesterday...
Country roads, take me home
to the place I belong.—John Denver

The coolness of the air made me shiver, yet sweat from my furrowed brow blurred my vision as I struggled to open my eyes. When I finally got them open, bright lights of many colors blinded me and forced my eyes shut once again.

I could sense movement around me, which compelled me to force my eyes to open once more. The bright lights and my blurred vision made it difficult to make out my surroundings. I watched as ghostly shadows on the walls danced about with spastic, yet graceful movements.

1

I lay on a surface that was translucent and unsupported, giving me a feeling of floating in the air.

In my blurred vision, I could make out a large circular device with multicolored lights positioned above my torso. Sharp pointed utensils protruded from the sphere. I had a feeling that I wasn't in a good situation, but was helpless to change it.

I felt naked under the snowy white cloth that covered most of my body. Strange high pitched eerie sounds reverberated in my mind. Sounds that were alien in nature.

Something lifted the cloth and started probing and prodding various parts of my anatomy. My inspector played with me as if I were its favorite doll.

An altered state of consciousness cloaked my mind as I began to laugh, then cry, and floated off to Disneyland, while the melody "It's a Small World" played in my mind. I had no idea what was so funny or sad. Nonetheless, tears poured from my eyes, further blurring and confusing my surroundings.

After doing whatever it was they had intended, my abductors implanted a memory block and a tracking device and sent me on my way. Their plan was now initiated. This would be my first abduction, but it wouldn't be my last. I would have no memory of them until many years later. Unknowingly, I would become a restless spirit on a endless flight.

This event occurred on a cool, crisp, clear autumn evening in 1960. I was heading back home after dumping the trash at the city dump a few miles north of town. There was no roadside trash pickup in those days. Taking the trash to the city dump had become my weekly chore since I'd turned seventeen and gotten a car.

Dad had found a mint-condition 1947 four-door Dodge sedan for a mere fifty bucks. It looked to be brand spanking new, with not a scratch on it. A widow had been storing it in her garage since her husband had passed away several years earlier.

I had been working a couple paper routes for the past few years and had saved up the money to pay for the car and the insurance. At my age, pedaling a bike was getting embarrassing. Dad finally decided I had matured enough to drive a car.

I named her Betsy. She was my pride and joy, but only for a day, as never in my wildness dreams, she would quickly turn into another embarrassment.

My first stop was to pull into a gas station.

"Whut'll it be?" Asked the attendant.

"Fill her up," I said, with a big smile on my face. You might say I was in seventh heaven and on cloud nine.

Not only did he fill her up, but the attendant checked the oil, the water in my radiator, and the air in my tires. He even cleaned the windows. You don't get that type of service in the future!

Later that evening, as I returned home from the city dump, I could see dust kicking up from the gravel road behind the car in the rearview mirror. The only sounds were those of the engine purring and the radio playing the "devil's music," which was what our parents were calling the new rock and roll sound. They were really going to come unglued when heavy metal would come out a few years down the road.

It was a peaceful evening, and there was not another car in sight. The stars were slowly making their appearance. There was no moon. I was dreaming about joining the navy in a few months, after I graduated from high school. My mind was a thousand miles away as I sailed the seven seas.

All of a sudden, out of nowhere, my little dream world evaporated as I noticed three blinking lights in my rearview mirror, rapidly approaching, in a tight formation. I couldn't tell if they were on the road or in the air. They approached with blazing speed, and in the blink of an eye I had something tailgating me.

What the heck? Not even Superman can travel that fast, I thought.

Dad burn it, some nut driving on my ass.

Hey asshole, back off.

For crying out loud, read the darn driver's manual. Ten miles an hour for one car length.

But who pays attention to the manual after they get their license? Certainly not the dude riding my tail.

You can tell that I'm getting a little pissed. I bet you can sense some road rage brewing here.

Suddenly, the car started to vibrate. I felt a tingling sensation and every hair on my body stood straight up. Before I could conceive what was happening, a humongous brilliant flash of colored light exploded within my head.

Confused and dazed, I realized the car was not moving.

How could that be?

Everything was still and quiet, except for the car engine, still purring, and the radio still playing that devil's music. I sat with my hands glued to the steering wheel. My grip was so tight that I could feel the muscles in my forearms tighten.

In the darkness I saw that the headlights were illuminating an embankment that ran alongside the road.

Holy cow! Whut in the world jest happened? I wondered.

I was shaking like a leaf on a cold windy day. The mind can play tricks in times of crisis, so I told myself to calm down and think. Because I was a teenager, thinking could sometimes be a new experience for me and could sometimes cause dangerous results, my folks had once told me.

Since the car's engine was still running, I decided I'd best haul ass and get on back home. The folks would be expecting me shortly.

I shifted to reverse and tried backing away from the embankment, but the rear tires would only spin. I began to smell burning rubber. This was not a good sign.

I realized that the front wheels were embedded in a ditch that ran along the embankment. I was not going anywhere.

Now whut?

I looked around inside the car and noticed some bizarre sights. The front and driver's side windows were smashed, making them resemble giant spider webs. I tried opening the driver's door, but it wouldn't budge.

I tried the passenger door. It was stuck too. I tried pushing on it with my shoulder. It wouldn't budge. Next I tried kicking it. It was being very contrary.

Frustrated, I crawled into the backseat. Both back doors were jammed shut too. I started to panic, and this made me mad. I kicked on both doors and cursed (good thing the folks couldn't hear me), but that didn't help, either. I still couldn't get any of the doors to budge.

Okay Tommy, pipe down and think.

I took a deep breath, told myself to relax, and decided to crawl back in front. There had to be a way to get out of the car. Good thing it wasn't on fire!

I tried to roll the window down. It was stuck. All the windows were stuck.

Lord, please help me.

That's when I again noticed the spider glass driver's side window. That just might be my escape route. After several kicks, each one a little harder than the last, and a few more curse words, the window finally gave way.

I crawled out of the car, staggered around a bit, and tried to collect my wits. I just happened to look to the sky and saw a full moon. Beside the moon were three small blinking lights, which flew off in formation and then disappeared into the night sky.

I didn't give what I saw much thought right then because when I looked at the car, I almost went into shock.

Holy shit!

I couldn't believe my eyes!

The moonlight and car's headlights lit up the area almost as if it were daylight. Betsy was a mess! She looked like something driven in a demolition derby, or something that had just came out of a junkyard!

Or maybe she had been out partying all night?

The first thing that stood out, like a sore thumb, was that the door handles were missing, both front and back. It appeared that they had been sawed off.

No wonder the doors wouldn't open.

The rest of the car was covered with dust, dents, and scrapes, front to back. The back fender was bent into the rear tire.

I walked around and inspected the car from several other angles. The back was perfectly normal, and the rear lights were still shining. The passenger side, however, looked the same as the driver's side. The door handles were missing, and the car was dented and scraped from front to back.

The front of the car also looked normal, except that the sun visor on the driver's side was crumbled and torn loose. Chrome strips were missing from nearly every part of Betsy. She was not a pretty sight.

Whut in the world could have caused all that damage?

I could only imagine what had happened. She had to have skidded on each of her sides, possibly turning over and landing back upright with her front wheels embedded in the ditch that ran alongside the road. If she had done all that, though, then how could I have stayed seated behind the steering wheel? The 1947 model automobiles had no seat belts or air bags.

None of this was making sense.

Since the car was still running, I figured I might as well try one more time to back out of the ditch. But first, I pulled the fender off the rear tire. I climbed back through the car window, put Betsy in reverse, and again tried backing up. The rear wheels spun and the smell of burning rubber once again filled the air. I tried rocking the car, to no avail. The front wheels were too deep in the ditch.

What am I going to do now?

As you can imagine, I was fit to be tied.

I had run out of ideas and had just about given up hope when I noticed a set of headlights coming down the road towards me.

"Need some help, sonny?" Asked a farmer, sitting on his tractor.

"Yes, sir. I sure do. Think yew cun pull my car out of the ditch?" I asked.

"Let's give it a shot," the farmer said.

Thank God, he had a chain. I helped him hook it to the car's fender, and the tractor pulled Betsy out quite easily.

"Jesus, sonny, whut in God's name happened here?" He asked, after surveying the car.

"Guess I must of had an accident," I replied.

"You don't say! The road's done torn up near half a mile back. There's debris scattered a 'bout everywhere," he said, as he shook his head in disbelief.

"Can't imagine how the darn thing is still a-runnin'."

"Yeah, me either," I said.

"Don't look like yew is hurt none," he said, as he looked me over.

"Reckon not," I replied, even though I felt my left elbow stiffening up.

"Must of been yew'en headlights I saw a-shinin' in the sky back yonder. I wuz a-wonderin' where those strange lights were a-comin' from. Yew is one lucky kid," the farmer said as he scratched his head.

"I reckon so. Much obliged for your help. I best be a-gettin' back home," I replied.

"No problem, boy. Yew jest best take it slow now. No tellin' whut else might fall off."

"Yes, sir. I will," I said. "My pa will be a-wonderin' why I've been gone for so long."

The farmer climbed back on his tractor and putted on down the road. I could hear him mumbling to himself. Somethin' about 'city folks'.

I climbed back through the busted window and started the dreaded trip home.

Shit, how am I ever going to explain this to dad, when I can't explain it to myself? I wondered.

It would be many years before I was to discover what had actually happened.

Just as I came to the city limits, I passed a police car parked alongside the road, facing in my direction. As I passed, going real slow, the officer looked up. He probably couldn't believe what he saw. His eyes got real big and he started choking on the bite of sandwich he had just taken.

All I could think to do was wave: "Evenin', Officer Cooper." He must have been real hungry, because I made it home without him pursuing me.

Teenagers tend to hide things from their folks. That seems to be a common occurrence in every generation. What the folks don't know won't hurt them, or more, properly put, what the folks don't know won't hurt the teenager. Unfortunately, there would be no way I could hide this from my folks. I sat in the driveway for a few minutes, working up my nerve to go into the house.

As soon as I opened the front door, Dad was on me like a fly on shit.

"Where's yew been, Bud? It's been darn't near three hours since you left," he hollered at me. (Dad always called me 'Bud' when I was in a heap of trouble).

Three hours! I hadn't realized it had been that long.

"I had a little car accident," I weakly confessed.

"An accident!" He shouted, as he rushed outside to see what I was talking about. The expression on his face, when he saw the car, would have stopped a grandfather clock.

"Whut in Sam Hill happened?" He asked.

"Don't really know, Pop. Maybe I hit a pothole and it caused the car to turn over," I lied, grasping at a straw.

"You is not hurt?"

"No, I don't think so," I replied.

"Well, it's way past your bedtime boy. We'll talk 'bout this in the mornin'," he said, still shaking his head and mumbling something I didn't quite hear, except for the word, "teenagers."

As I prepared to take a bath (we had no shower in those days), I noticed dried blood on my left shirt sleeve. I looked at my elbow and arm, but saw no blood. In the mirror I could see a two-inch scratch on my elbow. It wasn't bleeding and looked to be almost healed. Then I remembered the car's smashed side door window. My elbow must have hit it.

So why was there blood only on the shirt and not my arm? And the scratch looked to be almost healed?

Also in the mirror, I noticed that my right upper forearm was bruised. Looking closer, I saw a pattern that resembled the hand print of a small child, but there were just three fingers and a thumb. I noticed the exact same bruise and pattern on my left forearm.

I sat on the stool and bent down to untie my tennis shoes. At first I couldn't get them untied. They were tied in a strange and unfamiliar knot. I finally figured out how to get the knot undone and removed my shoes and socks.

I noticed that my left big toe was tender, and I saw that it was bruised. I sure didn't remember stubbing it. I reminded myself that I had just been in an accident, so I was bound to have a few bumps and bruises.

A few years later I developed a toenail fungus on that same toe. I would eventually discover that was where the abductors implanted the tracking device.

As I removed my undershirt and underpants, I noticed that the labels were on the outside. I had been wearing them inside out.

How had that happened? I must had been in a rush to get dressed that morning.

I was too tired to ponder the questions, so I took my bath and went to bed.

The next morning my folks noticed that I wasn't wearing my eyeglasses. I had had to wear them since the third grade. I thought I had them on, as I was seeing just fine. When I got them and put them on, my eyesight became blurred, as if I had them off. When I removed the glasses, it was if I had them on.

My parents thought I was joshing them, but when I read the headlines in the newspaper from across the room, they were convinced.

What the heck is goin' on here?

Whatever. It was a dream come true, cause I no longer had to be Tommy four eyes.

Also that morning, unbeknownst to me, the local radio station was reporting that several people had called and reported strange lights in the sky out by the city dump the night before.

Dad was as confused as I was about how a car could have almost the exact same type of damage on both sides and none on the front or back.

The next morning he drove out to examine the area where I told him I had had the accident. He was gone a long time. When he finally returned, all he said was, "Give me the car key. You're grounded." I reckon he didn't find any potholes.

The following morning, I awoke with blood in my underpants. Young boys my age were known to have wet dreams and I must have had a dilly. There was blood in my semen.

Mom discovered the blood while doing the laundry. I was taken to the doctor. He concluded that something must have been stuck up into my penis. My urethra seemed to be damaged. He said not to worry, as it would heal itself in a few days.

I had a hard time explaining to the folks that I had no idea what the doctor was talking about. Teenagers could do weird and stupid things, even in those days, but sticking something up my penis?

Come on, man. Give me a break.

I cringed just thinking about it.

A week later dad returned the car keys. He had fixed the car enough for it to be street legal to drive. Since I would be leaving for the navy in the spring, he couldn't see spending the money to fix the dents and scrapes. Betsy became known as the *Bad Mobile*, but as bad as she looked, there was no way I was going back to pedaling the bike.

Dad never did tell me what he found when he went to check the accident area. He must have found something, because when I asked him about it years later, he got the strangest look on his face. He stared off into space, probing for an answer. After what seemed like an eternity, he looked me straight in the eye and asked, "How can I explain something that I don't understand?" We never talked about the incident again.

Behold: The Comeback Kid's legacy is born.

CHAPTER TWO

THE INAUGURATION

NEW KID IN TOWN

Great expectations, everybody's watching you. Johnny come lately,
the new kid in town. Everybody loves you, so don't let them down…
Everybody's talking about the new kid in town. —The Eagles

Every story has a beginning. Mine starts with a twinkle in my
Daddy's eye.

I was born Thomas Leonard Hay, on April 15, 1943, at the
University of Kansas Hospital in Kansas City, Kansas. My surname
descended from William de la Haye, Butler of Scotland. In ancient
times the use of a badge or sign was used to mark a tribe or individual.
A family might revere a plant or tree because it was the plant of its
God. The Hay clan plant badge was a mistletoe.

If you should venture to Scotland—here are a few Scottish words that may come in handy:

"Scummindooncatzzandugs," which means: "The rain is indeed quite heavy."

"Sslikedeedawinter," which means: "This summer weather is like the Alps in winter."

"Achawishwidd-steyedathame," which means: "We should have stayed home."

My grandfather was Elijah Monroe Hay and my father was Leonard Monroe Hay. One of my favorite celebrities would be Marilyn Monroe. Remember the name Monroe. It will characterize my legacy.

Mom and Dad were separated at the time. It had something to do with the world at war. Dad was an aircraft mechanic in the Army Air Force, stationed in England. He received a few days leave to come home and see me when I was about six months old. After that, he didn't see me again until after the war.

Following the war, my parents settled in Clinton, Missouri, where dad had been raised. Clinton was a small town in Henry County, known as the Golden Valley. In the 1950s, Clinton was the baby chick capital of the world. 110 million chicks were hatched there annually. Clinton's fresh air and pure natural water provided the ideal climate for producing healthy chicks.

Clinton was also known for having the third-largest business "square" in the world. It was a typical small Midwestern town, where everyone knew everything about everyone else. There were no secrets in Clinton, or were there?

RUNAWAY

> *As I walk along, I wonder what went wrong. Tears*
> *are fallin' and I feel the pain.*—Del Shannon

"Come on, Flip," I shouted at the mangy mixed-breed mutt following me. There weren't many pure breed dogs in those days.

He wagged his tail as he caught up with his friend. I don't know why, but at the age of four, I was running away from home. This would be my first memory.

I was walking down the middle of the railroad tracks, about a half mile outside of town, carrying a small pillowcase packed with my meager belongings. I had no idea where I might be headed or from what I was running. I just knew I had to get away.

"There he is! We found him," I heard someone shout in the distance.

"Tommy, where yew think yew is a-goin'?"

Grandpa had noticed I was missing and had the whole family out looking for me. I couldn't understand what all the fuss was about when they found me. Nobody seemed to care about me, so I had figured I wouldn't be missed. After all, I was just one of many mouths my grandparents had to feed.

My relatives were in a panic because just a few months earlier, two children about my age had wandered off in the same area and had drowned in a pond nearby. Everyone was relieved that I was safe, but after the dust had settled, it didn't keep me from getting my first whupplin'.

THE WAY WE WERE

Memories, like the corners of my mind. Misty water-colored memories of the way we were.—Barbara Streisand

Within the next four years, Mom and Dad gave me three sisters, Sandra, Barbara, and Susan. The folks must then have discovered what was causing all the siblings, because after Susan there were no more. Or so I was led to believe at the time.

We were raised in a house across the street from Franklin Elementary School. The school playground became our own private playground. It was an ideal location to raise a family.

The neighborhood kids played all sorts of games, including marbles, lids, red rover, London Bridge, horseshoes, hopscotch, basketball, dodge ball, kick the can, football, and my favorite, baseball. We would spend hours doing the hula hoop. Very few of us were overweight, because we didn't sit inside and play video games all day. All our games were reality games.

We climbed trees and caught lightening bugs and even honey bees in our bare hands. The challenge with the bees was to keep from getting stung. I lost the challenge more than once.

In the third grade my teacher noticed me squinting when looking at the blackboard. She told my parents that I should get my eyes checked. Sure enough, I was nearsighted. I became Tommy four-eyes and started feeling like an ugly duckling. Not many kids had to wear glasses in those days, so I was constantly teased about them.

Why, I wondered, *was I the only one in the family with poor eyesigh*t?

However, it didn't stop me from playing my favorite sport.

IT'S ALL IN THE GAME

Many a tear has to fall, but it's all in the game.—Nat King Cole

IOOF Team Having Uphill Struggle, read the sports headlines in the local newspaper, *The Clinton Eye*. "We're not winning many games, but the boys are improving," said our little league manager, Don Blystone. He agreed that the main objective was to develop sportsmanship, but suggested it would be good for team morale to win a game occasionally. In those days we kids played with our folks yelling and screaming *for* us, not *at* us.

Baseball was the love of my life growing up. Even today it is still my favorite sport. At the age of seven, I became a diehard St. Louis Cardinals fan. They were the only professional baseball team west of the Mississippi. My grandpa got me hooked on them, and we listened to many of their games on the radio together.

There it goes. It might be, it could be, IT IS, A HOME RUN! HOLY COW, Harry Caray would shout. Stan "The Man" Musial hit five homers in the doubleheader that day in 1954.

Baseball was my outlet for a serious problem that was arising.

BAD MOON RISING

> *I see the bad moon arising. I see trouble on the way. I see hurricanes and lightning. I see bad times today...There's a bad moon on the rise.*—Credence Clearwater Revival

Everyone had chores. My main chore was mowing the lawn with a push mower. We had a big lawn and it seemed to take forever to mow. I would visit the house in my adult years and couldn't believe how much smaller the lawn was than I remembered it.

Sometimes, by mistake, I would mow over Mom's flowers. Some of them looked like weeds to me. Honestly, they did. Of course, I couldn't convince Mom of this, and she would get mad at me. But then, Mom seemed to be upset with me no matter what I did. I just couldn't do anything to please her. I started to believe that she didn't like me, but I couldn't understand why.

Maybe, I thought, *it was because I was the oldest, the only boy, or the ugly duckling.*

I hardly ever heard my folks argue, but when they did, it was always about me. I never heard them arguing about my sisters. It seemed they could do no wrong. In any disputes I had with my sisters, Mom would always side with them. I started to feel like I was the black sheep of the family.

However, at the time, I wasn't aware of all the circumstances my folks were dealing with. My differences with Mom even led me to believe that she was trying to do me harm, at one point.

Clinton had one public swimming pool. One day, Mom decided to teach me to swim. Instead of holding me up, though, it seemed to me that she was trying to drown me.

In a panic, I started screaming, "Help! Help! She's trying to drown me."

That raised a few eyebrows.

This must have made her mad because she did dunk me. From this point on, I would never get close to her again while in the water. I was becoming fearful of her in more ways than one.

FAMILY TRADITION

> *Country music singers have always been a real close family…I am very proud of my daddy's name… It's a family tradition.* —Hank Williams Jr.

The entire family came to the dinner table for meals. We always ate at home. None of us had ever heard of McDonalds or fast food. Fast food was when you were in a hurry to eat so you could get back outside to play. The call for dinner wasn't on a cell phone. Dad whistled. You'd best be in range and come a 'runnin' or you would go hungry.

Mom decided what we ate and prepared the meals. If I didn't like what she put on my plate, I was allowed to sit there until I did. Everyone's plate had to be clean before anyone could be excused.

Dinner was also a time to share the day's events. However, it was wise to watch what you said. It wasn't a good idea to go puttin' your foot in your mouth and get yourself in a fix.

We had no air conditioning, only fans to circulate the hot air. There was no shower, except when it would rain. We had to take a bath once a week, whether we needed it or not. We had to share the same bath water.

Since I was the only boy, or probably because I was always the dirtiest, I went last. My sisters would torment me, saying that they had peed in the water. I could only hope that they were lying, since I had no other choice. But I'd get my revenge by putting bugs in their beds. Their horrendous shrieks had me grinning ear to ear. :)

We didn't have a TV until I was fourteen, and when we did get one it was a black-and-white, nineteen-inch RCA model that seemed to take forever to warm up. There were two stations, and they went off the air at midnight, after playing the national anthem and a poem about God. The stations would come back on the air at 6:00 a.m. Strange how now days there are over four hundred channels that broadcast around the clock, and I can't seem to find anything worthwhile to watch.

Can you believe that someone had to actually get off their butt to adjust the sound or change channels? Some of my favorite programs were: *The Lone Ranger, Twilight Zone, Superman, Red Skelton, and The Rifleman.*

The first movie I saw was *Love Me Tender.* Elvis had all the silly girls screaming so much that I could barely hear the movie. The world news and a cartoon were shown before the movie. There were no advertisements, previews, or trailers.

Mom bought our clothes. I never had any say in what I wore. I wore it or went naked. But then, naked wasn't really a choice. I wore the same pair of jeans until they were full of holes and about to fall apart. I should have saved them. My grandkids today would have paid dearly for them.

The folks didn't have to put up with fagging. After all, who would be so stupid as to make it easier for them to swat your butt? Not I. They swatted mine enough without me inviting them.

To mail a letter cost ten cents. Twenty-five cents bought a malt at the Dairy Queen. Black walnut was my favorite. Gas for the car was twenty-nine cents a gallon. Haircuts were fifty cents. The monthly grocery bill was around a hundred dollars. Families lived on one parent's income and had only one car. You're probably wondering how in the world we ever survived.

Only one rotary-dial telephone hung from the wall, and it had a party line. If another party happened to be on the line when you wanted to make a call, you'd have to wait until they were finished.

We always had to ask permission just to look at the phone. It had to of been a dumb phone though, because they invented smart ones in the future.

To do anything or go anywhere, I had to ask permission. Dad would take forever to make up his mind.

Patience grasshopper.

I wasn't aware of it at the time, but I suppose he was teaching me patience.

T'was the night before Christmas and all through the house, anxious little creatures were stirring, along with the mice. Thanks to our parents, Christmas was always a special time of year. They always managed to surprise us. Dad probably spent most of the night assembling the toys. We each got two, or at the most three, presents each year.

There was no chimney for Santa, so we had to leave the front door unlocked. But then, I can't remember the front door or any other door in the house ever having a lock.

Every Memorial Day the entire family, including grandparents, uncles, aunts, and cousins, would travel to Springfield, Missouri, to visit and put flowers on family members' graves. Afterwards, everyone would gather at Uncle Perry's. He and grandpa would play the fiddle and everyone would dance.

Dad's side of the family would get together at his parents' (my grandparents) home, at least once a month. They lived on a farm a few miles south of Clinton. There were many cousins to play with. I did a lot of hunting and fishing. Grandma would cook our game, but it was her chicken and dumplings that I liked best.

It was at their farm that I would get into another situation that would cause me bodily harm. All the cousins were playing a game of Cowboys and Indians one day. I was an Indian. The cowboys were holed up in the middle of a field, in a fort made from bales of hay. The Indians found it impossible to sneak up on them without being seen, so I came up with a brilliant plan: "Let's burn 'em out!" At that the field was set on fire.

That didn't go over so well, as the adults all came running out of the house when someone yelled "FAHR!" Everyone grabbed at a water hose and started straying the fire.

"Who started that fahr?" Grandpa soon asked.

The next thing I knew, all fingers were pointing at yours truly.

"Tommy did it," they all shouted.

There was nowhere to run or hide.

That little adventure got me a few welts on my behind and a stern scolding in front of all my relatives.

Don't get the wrong idea here, it's not that I was a bad kid growing up. I was just a little adventurous, or ornery, as some would say. It would be a trait that plagues me to this day.

Some might wonder where that might have came from, and what might have caused it? Maybe feeling a little unwanted had something to do with it. But then, maybe not.

So to keep out of trouble, I played a lot of baseball.

I played mostly in Little League and Babe Ruth. My parents never drove me to my games. I had a bicycle that seemed to weigh thirty pounds, and it had only one slow speed. However, I would attach a card between the spokes of the wheels to make it sound like a motorcycle and defiantly made it go faster.

It also made me a cool dude!

I pedaled that bike until I was seventeen. I don't know how many miles I put on it, but it was a bunch, as I rode it everywhere I went.

The folks would send me and my sisters to church every Sunday. I suppose it was the only time they could be alone. Had no idea why they would want to be alone.

They wouldn't let me ride my bike, as I had to escort my sisters. We would walk the five blocks to the First Christian Church. My sisters would embarrass me with their little girl "silliness," which inspired me to walk a half block behind them. I didn't want anyone thinking that I was associated with such 'silly creatures'.

Hey, Tommy, everyone in town knows you're related.

It still made me to want to run away and hide.

The only times I ever left the state of Missouri growing up were when we would visit Mom's relatives in Connecticut. We would travel by automobile for the three-day journey. It was exciting to travel on the turnpike and through the many tunnels along the way.

Entertaining four kids sitting in the backseat of a car for three days had to be stressful on the folks. Counting farm animals and then losing them when we passed a graveyard, quickly became boring. That's when the bickering would start.

"Tommy touched me."

"She touched me first."

" Stop it!"

There was constant bickering. I can remember more than once, Dad stopping alongside the highway, pulling one of us out of the car, and whipping our butt. This would quiet things down for a few miles, but then we'd be right back at it again.

"Tommy touched me."

No wonder both parents smoked and Dad lost most of his hair by the age of forty.

Thank God we didn't grow up in today's society, because if the ACLU had existed, Dad would had been arrested and gone to prison for child abuse. All of us kids would have been raised separately in foster homes. No telling how we would have turned out.

Basically, you could say kids in those days were in fear for their well-being, but it wasn't because of child abuse, drive-by, mall, theater, school shootings, drugs, or gangs. The fear of dad's belt or a switch cut from the branch of a tree was what kept us in line.

There were no time-outs, groundings, or stress cards to flash. We took our lickings, and I'll be darn, we kept on ticking. Our parents and grandparents were a much bigger influence than in today's society, where most kids are now raised by babysitters and teachers.

There were hardly any step and half relatives in those days. Never heard of a thing called 'tough love'.

Maybe a whooping now and then wasn't so bad after all. Lo and behold, maybe we survived because our parent's love was greater than their threat.

AGAINST ALL ODDS

> *Take a look at me now, 'cause there's just
> an empty space.*— Phil Collins

December 27, 1958, is a date that will always be embedded in my mind. I can still picture, in slow motion, the BB floating toward and then smashing the right lens of my eyeglasses. The event was reported in the local newspaper:

> *PATROL AND KC POLICE AID IN MERCY MISSION—
> Tommy Hay, 14, has undergone a harrowing experience
> since Friday. He and his friend were playing with
> their BB guns, when a pellet shattered the right lens,
> causing glass fragments to enter both eyes.*

> *The youth was taken to Wetzel Hospital, where Dr. R.
> J. Powell removed some of the glass. Dr. Powell then
> recommended that Tommy transfer to Dr. White, an
> eye specialist in Sedalia, Mo.*

> *Dr. White removed more glass and then recommended
> that Tommy be transferred again. This time to a
> Kansas City eye specialist, because some of the glass
> particles were too deeply embedded in the eyes.*

> *The trip to the Kansas City hospital took until 1:30
> a.m. Tommy's parents had high praise for the Missouri
> State Highway Patrol and the KC Police Department.*

The excited and worried parents experienced great difficulty in driving through one of the worst snow storms to hit this area in decades. They had to contact the Highway Patrol and get snow chains installed on the car's wheels. The patrol had to order another car off the station's grease rack. The patrol then escorted the family to the city limit, where the Lee's Summit police met and escorted them to the hospital.

Treatment started immediately upon arrival to remove the remaining glass fragments. The surgery was successful in saving Tommy's eyesight.

After the surgery, the doctor explained that he had to leave a fragment of glass in one eye. It was buried too deep, and removing it would be too risky. He said that leaving it in the eye should not cause any problems.

REUNITED

I was a fool to ever leave your side. Me minus you is such a lonely ride.—Peaches and Herb

It was almost Halloween, and behold, a wicked witch from the North came a-callin'. It would be a day that rocked my little world upside down and inside out. But it would also be a day of reconciliation.

"Tommy, Tommy! Stop!" I heard someone yell.

I was delivering the *Clinton Democrat* newspaper on my route as usual that day when a lady came running out of a house, shouting my name. I was around fifteen years old.

"Stop! I want to talk to you," she shouted again.

Now, I always tried to throw the paper as close to the front porch as possible, but sometimes one would go astray, so I figured I was going to catch hell for one landing in the bushes, or a mud puddle. I stopped, expecting to get scolded.

"Tommy, I am your mother," she said.

Whut? My mother? Did she jest say she wuz my mother? I thought. *Or maybe she said she knew my mother?*

"Tommy, I am your mother and I want to talk with you," she repeated as she came running toward me.

Time stood still. I stood there dumbfounded.

Must be something wrong with my hearing.

Why would this strange woman claim to be my mother? I'd never seen her before in my life.

Scared shitless, I finally snapped out of my trance and took off, like a bat out of hell, thinking that this woman must be some kind of a witch. I suspected she wanted my hide for her witches brew.

I looked back over my shoulder to make sure she hadn't hopped on her broom to chase me down. But she was just standing there, watching me high-tail it down the street like a scared jackrabbit.

Now this kind of shook me up, as you might imagine. For the rest of my route and all the way home, I couldn't shake how she looked and what she had said. I didn't say anything to anybody when I got home, but I lay awake most of the night wondering why this strange witchy woman would claim to be my mother.

The next day on my route, at the same house, the witch swept upon me again. She was a restless spirit on an endless flight.

"Tommy, Tommy, please stop. I just want to talk to you. I'm your mother," she said again.

Now I was totally convinced that this woman had to be a witch. I put the pedal to the metal and ski-daddled out of there before sparks could fly from her finger tips.

But that evening, at the dinner table, I worked up the nerve to tell the folks what had happened in the past two days.

All of a sudden, it got very quiet. I mean real quiet. You could have heard a pin—or maybe even a feather—hit the floor. Finally,

Mom broke the silence when she started choking on the bite of food she had just taken.

"How cun Tommy have another mother?" My oldest sister Sandy asked.

"Girls, go to your rooms," mom shouted.

"But we haven't finished eatin'," all the girls said.

"I said go to your rooms. NOW!" Shouted mom again.

She then looked at Dad and said, "Suppose it's time we told him."

"Tell me whut," I cried, having no idea what they could be referring to.

Dinner and my life were interrupted that evening, as a whole new world was revealed to me. As it turned out, the witch was my mother.

Now, how could that be, you ask?

The mom I knew was actually my stepmom. Ok. Someone has a lot of explaining to do.

Dad explained that during the war he and my birth mother had divorced, right after I was born. I was only two years old when my birth mother dropped me off ("abandoned me," were his words) with his parents in Clinton. He said that my birth mom no longer wanted to be bothered with me, since another man had come into her life, while dad was stationed in England. (I would eventually learn that he had stretched the truth at bit with those statements).

In his quivering voice, I heard the hatred he felt toward my birth mom, as he struggled to explain things to me. Grandpa had raised me until he returned home from the war. Dad said he had met my stepmom in England and they were married after the war. I was too young to remember all this.

My birth mother's Aunt lived on my paper route and must have recognized me. She informed my birth mom, who at the time was living in Kansas City. My birth mom desired to reconnect with me, so that started the whole chain of events.

Wow! I hadn't seen that one coming. I discovered that my sisters and I had different mothers.

Things started to fall into place now, and made more sense. I now began to understand why mom had been treating me differently. Perhaps this could explain some of the bad feelings between us.

Could I have been a thorn in her side?

I was definitely part of a ready-made family.

Come to find out, I looked a lot like my birth mom, so maybe every time my stepmom looked at me, she saw that other woman.

Ouch! That had to be painful.

There must have been some contact between Dad and birth mom soon after she surprised me, because before I knew it, she was coming to our home to visit me. She was allowed to come into the living room and sit with me, while the rest of the family moved to another room. Talk about feeling awkward. I didn't know this woman, and what little I had heard about her was real bad. I had no idea what to call her. She told me her name was Kathryn. I was frightened and very uncomfortable in her presence. I certainly wasn't much for conversation.

The visits didn't last long. Dad told me her visitations were disrupting our family atmosphere. I was encouraged to write her a letter and say that I wasn't interested in a relationship with her. There really wasn't much of a choice on my part. The family that I knew was my life, and this other woman was a complete stranger. Kathryn respected my (dad's) wish, and I had no more contact with her until after I joined the navy.

My folks never apologized for keeping this secret from me. I never did discover if or when they had planned to tell me. I suppose they had their reasons. I would discover in my senior years that they hadn't even told their closest friends. Relatives that knew had been told to keep their mouths shut about this little secret.

THE WAYWARD WIND

*The wayward wind is a restless wind, a restless wind
that yearns to wander. And he was born the next of kin,
the next of kin to the wayward wind.*—Gogi Grant

Not too long after this, another bombshell exploded and left another big crater in my little corner of the world. A few months after I met my birth mother, as I walked to my next ninth grade class, this scrawny kid who looked like a scarecrow called out my name.

"Tommy," he said, "don't yew know that we is brothers?"

This stopped me dead in my tracks.

Why in the world would this clown claim to be my brother?

All I could think to say was, "My brother? Yew is got to be nuts."

I had seen this kid before but had never talked to him. He was in the seventh grade and lived on the other side of the tracks. It was an unwritten law that you never associated with people from the other side of the tracks, because they were either poor or colored folks.

This kid had a ducktail haircut and wore a black leather jacket. Good kids had flat-top haircuts and wore turtleneck sweaters.

Fortunately, the bell rang for my next class, so I hurried off, eager to put some space between us. For the rest of the day, though, I kept wondering why this kid would claim to be my brother. Could there be another surprise awaiting out there somewhere?

That evening at the dinner table, I related what had happened at school that day.

Dead silence again. Of course it was my oldest sister, Sandy, who broke the silence. She was always the inquisitive one.

"How cun Tommy have a brother?" She asked.

I think Mom and Dad were about to have a cow, from the look on their faces. Finally Dad said, "Finish your dinner. We will talk about this later."

Not a word was spoken for the rest of the meal. It wasn't a golden silence as I could mentally hear everyone's thoughts ticking away.

After dinner, Dad took me out to the front porch. "Well, son, this kid, Mike's his name, jest so happens to be your half-brother."

Wow! I had a brother! I had always had a secret desire to have a brother!

Dad explained how this had come to be.

Mike was the son of my birth mother and her current husband, the man she supposedly ran off with when she left me at Grandpa's.

But he was a bad kid, dad explained, and I wasn't to have anything to do with him. Wow! I had a brother there for a minute, and then I was back to having no brother the next.

That's all he would tell me that night. I began to wonder just how many more relatives might pop out of the woodshed. These days, with the milkman going door to door, you didn't know who your siblings were anymore.

Remember now, this was Clinton, a small Midwestern town in the fifties. Bet some of you are probably starting to wonder if it wasn't really Peyton Place.

PUPPY LOVE

And they called it puppy love. Oh I guess they'll never know, how a young heart really feels. That's why they call it puppy love. —Paul Anka

Here she comes!

Oh boy, I got so excited it felt like I was about to pee my pants. Johanna was walking down the sidewalk, on the other side of the street, towards my house. She was so pretty, with her short cropped brown hair and sparkling brown eyes. Her infectious smile gave me a happy face that burnt bright red. The heat generated could melt homemade ice cream.

My heart would beat faster and I would get goose bumps at the very sight or thought of her. We were sophomore classmates, but she made all the other girls in our class look a lot younger. She was the reason I started noticing there was indeed a difference between boys and girls.

I dove for the bushes, because it was an excellent vantage point from which to watch her pass without being seen. She lived up the street and would pass our house on the way to the grocery store. I would watch her every move until she vanished from sight.

I never got the courage to even say "hi" to her. If only I'd had a cell phone, I could had at least have texted her. No telling how that would have changed our relationship.

But then, maybe not, because after our sophomore year, her family moved out of town. I never saw or heard of her again. She never knew how much of an effect she had on me. I reckon you could say she was a *puppy love.*

SLOW POKE

You keep me waiting 'til it's getting aggravating…
You're a slow poke.—Poco

It must have been a combination of zits, four eyes, and low self-esteem that made me feel so insecure in my teens. I was extremely shy and totally uncomfortable around girls.

The first time I ever held hands with a girl was in the eighth grade, and it certainly wasn't by choice. The teacher caught me pestering a girl. Why I would be pestering a girl was beyond me. My punishment was to sit beside her in class and hold her hand.

Yuck! Hold hands with a girl. I don't think so.

There you go thinking again, Tommy.

Now this was before Johanna, so I wasn't into girls yet, and this turned out to be pure torture. But I was no dummy, and came up with a brilliant solution.

Sitting in the back of the classroom, the teacher couldn't see us all that well. My Aunt Helen had given me a baseball glove for my birthday, so I put it to a better use that day. This required the girl to hold onto the glove instead of my hand.

Pretty clever, huh?

Until the teacher discovered my not so brilliant tactic.

Back in those days the teachers were allowed to swat students on their behinds with a wooden paddle. The paddles had holes drilled in them, no less. So I got swatted, right in front of the entire class. Talk about embarrassment! There went my face, lighting up like a Christmas tree full of red lights.

My family would have become rich if that had happened in today's society. The teacher would have been arrested and lost her job, while being labeled as a sexual predator. I'd have been tested for AIDS and given huge doses of Ritalin. You would have probably seen me in Michael Jackson's *Thriller* video, as I would have grown up to be a zombie.

The folks tried to help me out of my shyness. A few times they would drop me off at teen town. Teen town was where teens congregated, since malls hadn't been developed yet. Mostly I just hung around with a few guy friends and we would ogle the girls. You'll have to use your imagination to figure out how we did that, without a computer, cell phone, or IPad.

I had one other crush after Johanna. Her name was Jenny and she was the most pretty and popular girl in school, as well as the Homecoming Queen. I did kiss her on her cheek one day, *in my dreams.*

I had developed an eye for the pretty ones at a young age. I just didn't know what to do about it then. But, rest assured, I would eventually figure it out.

There would be a couple other occasions where my folks would suspect and accuse me of being with a girl. *Now how in the world could that be?*

HANKY-PANKY

*I never saw her, never really saw her. My baby
does the hanky panky.*—Tommy James

"Oh my God! Dad, you'd better come look at this," Mom screamed one day while she was doing the laundry.

Next thing I knew, Dad ordered me to remove my jeans and underwear.

What could I possibly have done now? I wondered.

I figured another whuppin' was a-comin' and I had no idea why.

I was somewhat relieved, but totally confused, when he only wanted to look at my private parts. Mom had noticed little bugs (crabs) crawling in my underwear. I had been itching in that area for a few days, but never thought to look for what caused it.

"Yew've been with a woman, haven't yew?" Dad asked.

I had absolutely no idea what he was talking about. He then explained what those little bugs were and how I must have gotten them. I think dad was aware that I was no ladies' man, so he figured it had to be something else.

The only logical explanation had to be that I had picked them up from a toilet seat at school. I had to shave and powder myself for a few days, until they disappeared.

To think girls could infest me with those type of little critters just made me even more leery of them.

LIPSTICK ON YOUR COLLAR

Told a tale on you, boy. Told me you were untrue.—Connie Francis

I know you are going to find this hard to believe, but I was suspected of being with a girl one other time. Mom found what she thought was lipstick on my coat collar. I just let her think that, because the truth would have been very painful for me. I knew it wasn't lipstick. It was a cherry brandy stain.

The night before, I had gotten my first taste of alcohol. It was too much for me to handle, as I was drinking it like soda pop. It hit me hard and fast. I got sicker than a dog, puked all over the place, and stained my coat collar. Never touched that stuff again while I was in high school.

FOR THE GOOD TIMES

Let's just be glad we had some time to spend together.—Hank Snow

I never got bored during my childhood, but it seemed to take forever to grow up. Then, when I did, it was way too fast and I wanted to be a kid again. Go figure.

Without video games, cell phones, or computers, I bet you're wondering how we occupied ourselves. My buddy Roger and I would listen to what our folks called *the devil's music*. It was a new rock and roll sound that had teenagers twitching in uncanny ways. We listened to it on the local radio station or played it on forty-five rpm records in Roger's garage. The folks thought we would surely grow up to be dysfunctional.

Another buddy, Frank, and I would use sticks of dynamite like firecrackers. Frank worked in a hardware store that sold dynamite sticks. He would borrow a few sticks now and then. We would toss some out the *bad mobile* window, while cruising the countryside. A farmer's mailbox must have got in the way and was blown to kingdom come one day. We heard on the radio later that the police were looking for vandals terrorizing the countryside. They even talked about bringing in the FBI, since destruction of a mailbox was a federal offense. That put an abrupt halt to that little amusement.

Frank and I played another game on the telephone, when the folks weren't home. We'd dial a random number and pretend to be the disc jockey from the local radio station. If the person we called could answer a question correctly, they would win a big prize, we told them. Our favorite question was: "How many drops of water flow over Niagara Falls every minute?"

Of course, they wouldn't have any idea, so we'd tell them to take a guess. When they guessed an answer, we would say, "Oh my gosh! You're absolutely right! Come on down to the station and collect your prize."

That little entertainment came to a screeching halt, too, when we heard the station was contacting the police to prosecute the perpetrators. Good thing caller ID hadn't been invented yet.

Bad boys, bad boys, what ya gonna do? What ya gonna do when they come for you?

Our favorite Halloween trick was putting dog, cow, or horse poop in a small paper bag. We then placed the bag at the front door of a residence. One of us would knock on the door, while the other would light the bag on fire. The resident would come to the door, spot the burning bag, and stomp on it to extinguish the fire. We learned a few new curse words doing that trick.

As you can see, it was a simple life, in simpler times. But that was about to drastically change. The Kid's childhood games would soon be replaced with grown-up games. Life was about to get a bit more complicated.

CHAPTER THREE

THE TRANSFORMATION

NO FUTURE IN THE PAST

How long do old memories last? Why can't I forget it? Why can't I admit it? There ain't no future in the past.—Vince Gill

The 1961 Clinton High Senior Class was the largest graduating class to date, with 136 students. After graduation, I had no desire to further my education. My grades had always been just high enough to get me to the next year. I never won any awards or got voted the best in anything, except maybe orneriness, by my parents.

However, my last semester in high school, I did make the Honor Roll, much to the surprise of my parents, my teachers, and even me. That was the semester following my freak accident out by the city dump. After that incident, my life, abilities, confidence and self-esteem would jump to another level.

I had always wanted to be an athlete, but never was good enough to make any of the school teams. However, that spring, I was finally able to outrun my best friend Roger. Up until then, he had always been able to beat me. He couldn't understand how I could all of a sudden outrun him. Neither could I, for that matter.

I even set a gym record for the 880 run that spring in my gym class. My gym coach tried to talk me into joining the high school track team, but I still hadn't yet found confidence within myself. Plus I had two jobs.

I was still shy around girls and would be too embarrassed to hold much of a worthy conversation with one.

What could be so embarrassing? After all, weren't they God's little creations of sugar, spice, and everything nice?

My parents and teachers never discussed the birds and bees with me. I graduated from high school having never been kissed and still a virgin. Can you imagine that in today's society? I'd be labeled a freak, geek, and a nerd, all rolled into one. Well, all this was about to change.

After graduation, I felt the urge to spread my wings and get out of Dodge. I couldn't explain why, I just knew I had to leave. Don't take it wrong. Clinton was a good place to be raised. Overall, I had a good upbringing. My parents didn't burden me with having to make many decisions. I didn't have to worry about what to eat, wear, or where to hang my hat. My biggest worry was about the weather cancelling a baseball game.

The folks taught me some very important aspects of life that would help me in the future:

LOGIC: *Because we said so, that's why!*

STAMINA: *You'll sit there until your plate is clean.*

CLEANLINESS: *You'll stay in your room until it's clean and the bed is made.*

ANTICIPATION: *Just wait until your father gets home.*

BECOMING AN ADULT: *If you don't eat your veggies, you'll never grow up.*

ROOTS: *Close the door. Were you born in a barn?*

IRONY: *Keep crying and I'll give you something to cry about.*

Nevertheless, I felt the urge be all I could be. The navy, not the army, provided the perfect opportunity. Looking back, I wonder if the abductors played a role in this decision?

IN THE NAVY

In the navy, yes, you can sail the seven seas, in the navy, yes, you can put your mind at ease. —Village People

Right after high school, my friend Roger and I joined the navy, on their *Buddy Program*. We were guaranteed to stay together throughout boot camp. Unfortunately for me, I sprained my left ankle badly the day before the physical in Kansas City. During my physical, the navy doctor noticed I was limping pretty badly. He turned me down because I'd never have made it through boot camp on a sprained and swollen ankle. He told me to try again when the ankle healed.

So Roger flew off to San Diego and I limped back to Clinton. I was devastated. After moping around for a month, I talked my buddy Frank into joining me on the same program. This time we both passed the tests.

Watch out world, the Kid was about to spread his wings and fly like an eagle.

The trip to San Diego would be my first time on an airplane, and my excitement level darn near reached the stars. In my excitement,

I had no clue about the shock and awe that awaited me. I was in for a rude awakening.

BEND ME, SHAPE ME

Bend me, shape me, anyway you want me. You got
the power to turn on the light. —Amen Corner

"WHAT THE FUCK YOU LOOKIN' AT, YOU PUSSY? YOU THINK I'M PRETTY? LINE UP! ASSHOLE TO BELLYBUTTON! DROP YOUR COCK AND GRAB YOUR SOCKS!"

"SIR, YES SIR!"

My parents would surely washed my mouth out with soap if ever I used such language.

"HUT TWO THREE FOUR. YOUR LEFT, YOUR LEFT RIGHT LEFT. YOUR OTHER LEFT, YOU MORON! STRAIGHTEN THAT LINE!"

Boot camp instructors started shouting at me as soon as I departed the bus. They knew only to yell and curse. I couldn't understand why they were so pissed off with me. I discovered quickly that there was absolutely nothing I could do that would ever pacify them. (And I had thought my stepmom was always mad at me for no reason. She had nothing on these guys.) I learned real quick to keep my mouth shut and to never volunteer for anything. Nothing I had ever experienced could have prepared me for the next nine weeks.

The San Diego Naval Base was gigantic, bigger than the whole town of Clinton. There were hundreds of recruits there trying to make the miraculous transformation from civilian to U.S. Navy sailor. It was a drastic metamorphosis, both mentally and physically.

Every week about thirty raw recruits, fresh out of high school, from various states, and thinking they could conquer the world, were thrown together to form a company. The company ate, slept, worked, marched, and trained together for the next nine weeks. The company needed to learn to function as a unit. If one person screwed up, the whole company suffered the consequences.

In the first week they instilled in us three words that have been with me and every recruit since: *Honor, Courage, and Commitment.* This is the U.S. Navy motto, and these were the core values that immediately became the ideals we lived by. I remember to this day an instructor telling us: *What you make of this experience is what will make you as a person.* He hit the nail right on the head.

In the second week, we went through the confidence course. This is designed to simulate emergency conditions aboard a warship. The instructors taught us to be sharp, to be self-reliant, and above all, to make key decisions upon which our shipmates might depend. Teamwork dominates and infiltrates every aspect of a sailor's life.

Week three put us onboard a land-bound training ship. We learned the name of nearly every working part of the ship. They taught us first-aid techniques and how to signal from ship to ship using flags. We spent a lot of time in the classroom learning navy customs and courtesies, the law of armed conflict, shipboard communications, ship and aircraft identification, and basic seamanship. All this was interspersed with physical training, including sit-ups, sit-reaches, and push-ups. Tons of push-ups!

During week four we got some weaponry training with the M14 rifle. We had to carry that sucker everywhere we went, including the head (bathroom). My hunting skills came in handy, as I earned a sharpshooter badge.

The firefighting and shipboard damage control course came next. Everyone learned how to extinguish fires, escape smoke-filled compartments, open and close water-tight doors, operate the oxygen breathing apparatus, and move and store fire hoses. It was during this training that I thought I might have met my Waterloo.

During an exercise simulating a compartment fire, the lead man on the hose panicked, dropped his position, and disappeared. I was in the second position and felt the hose start to sway. I could barely see my hand in front of my face through the smoke. My lungs were quickly filling with smoke and I heard the guys behind me choking too. I knew if we didn't get the fire out, we would have to try it again. No way did I want to do that. When the going gets tough, the tough get going. Somehow I managed to grab the front hose position and distinguish the fire.

The following week, the training exercise involved the confidence chamber. The whole company was put in a gas chamber with our gas masks on. The instructor then unleashed a tear-gas tablet. Everyone had to remove his mask and recite his name and serial number. This exercise was repeated until everyone got it right. I got it right the first time. Hey, there ain't no crying in baseball and most definitely not in the U.S. Navy.

During the last week of training everyone had to jump off a one-hundred-foot platform into the water and tread water for at least thirty minutes. It was surprising how many recruits joined the navy and didn't know how to swim. They learned that day or they were shipped out.

All recruits are tested, both physically and in aptitude. Physically, I discovered that my eye-to-hand coordination had improved immensely, compared to my pre-accident days. I could now do activities I never dreamed of doing before. My aptitude tests revealed that I had skills I never knew existed. My eyesight had even improved, so that I didn't need to wear glasses anymore. When I told the navy eye doctor about the fragment of glass left from the BB gun accident, he couldn't find anything in my eye. Somehow, it had disappeared.

I went from 135 pounds wet to 175 pounds of lean mean fighting machine. Why the sudden improvements? I gave most of the credit to the navy, since I had no reason to think otherwise.

I CAN SEE CLEARLY NOW

I can see clearly now, the rain is gone. I can see all obstacles in my way. Gone are the dark clouds that had me blind. —Johnny Nash

Graduation day was a proud day for all who made it through boot camp. Those of us left had proved we had the right stuff. We dressed in our brand new dress uniforms and paraded past all our instructors and the upper brass.

On the way to graduation, I passed a mirror and almost didn't recognize the dude staring back at me. I had found within myself a confidence and pride I had never known existed. For the first time in my life, I felt proud of myself. I had developed a completely different personality. Whatever had existed before was now gone. Tommy boy had become a man.

The navy gave me two weeks' leave after boot camp, so I went back to visit my parents and sisters. I was sitting on a bench at the bus station when they walked right past, looking for me. No one had recognized me.

"Hey guys, it's me, Tom."

"Is that really you, Tommy?" Asked my oldest sister, Sandy.

The expression on their faces was priceless.

The navy decided to send me to radioman school after boot camp. My aptitude tests had revealed that I had the skills to be a radioman. (Wonder where I got those from?) But first, they sent the FBI to my hometown for a background check. Radiomen would have access to top-secret data that is normally concealed from the public. They couldn't have a Russian spy or an alien infiltrating the ranks.

I received a top-secret clearance and was sent to the radioman school at the same base in San Diego where I had received my boot camp training. Luckily, the FBI didn't uncover the fireworks and telephone pranks, nor the abduction.

WESTERN UNION

A telegram was traveling on its way…Flashing across the darkness on the telegraph machine. —Kinky Friedman

"Fuck this shit," a classmate said as he picked up his typewriter, slammed it and his earphones to the floor, and walked out of the classroom, mumbling to himself. I never saw him again. He probably finished his naval career swabbing decks.

I guess listening to the dit-dah-dit of Morse code for four hours a day got nerve wracking for some. It would drive many a sane man right up a wall, but not me. I had no idea why, but it was music to my ears, and seemed to come naturally to me. For the first time in my life I accomplished something that most others struggled with. I even impressed the instructors. To graduate, a student had to achieve at least eighteen words a minute, both sending and receiving. I doubled that halfway through the course.

Radioman duties included ship-to-ship and ship-to-shore communications. In 1961 the main types of communications were voice, signal flags, Morse code, and crypto, using UHF and VHF frequencies. I learned each one of the communications methods, plus basic electronics.

I would think the abductors were proud of their prodigy.

BEYOND THE SEA

It's far beyond the stars, it's near beyond the moon…
happy we'll be beyond the sea. —Bobby Darin

After graduating at the top of my class, I received orders to join the aircraft carrier USS *Hancock*. At the time, she was on station in the Far East.

The history of ships bearing the name "Hancock" is as long and dramatic as the history of the U.S. Navy itself. During the period from 1775 through today, the national ensign has flown from three successive "Hancock's." Through the Revolutionary War and both world wars, a "Hancock" was in action.

The intrepid spirit of "Hancock" has inspired the present "Hancock" since her commissioning during World War II. Nicknamed the "Fighting Hannah" for her battle prowess, during the war she destroyed more than 730 enemy planes and 17 Japanese warships, 31 merchant ships, and 51 railroad trains. Fighting back after kamikaze hits, she won the navy unit commendation with the following citation: *For outstanding heroism in action against enemy Japanese forces in the air, ashore, and afloat. Operating continuously in the most forward areas, the USS Hancock and her groups struck crushing blows toward annihilating Japanese forces. Daring and dependable in combat, the Hancock rendered loyal service in achieving the ultimate defeat of the Japanese empire.*

In 1961, the USS Hancock still strived to keep the peace she'd fought so hard to win. Modernized with an angled wooden deck, the first steam catapults ever used on an American carrier, and mirror landing systems, she alternated every six months between pilot qualifications on the West Coast and deployments in the Far East as a member of the Seventh Fleet.

In crises such as those in Formosa, Quemoy and Matsu, Laos, and Vietnam, the men of the "Fighting Hannah" were ready, proving themselves worthy guardians of the proud tradition begun by the illustrious Massachusetts patriot who gave the ship her name.

To hook up with my new home, I flew from San Diego to Alaska to Japan, and then into Subic Bay, in the Philippines. My first trip outside the United States would produce a cultural shock.

The base at Subic Bay was just like an average town in the United States, but once you ventured outside the base, it was a completely different world. This was the filthiest place I had ever seen. To get into town, I had to cross a bridge over a river, where I saw naked children swimming in sewage.

The town consisted of one main street lined with nothing but hotels and nightclubs.

"Hey, Sailor Boy, you want date?" Asked half-naked, sexy, pretty Filipino girls. Most didn't look a day over sixteen.

Every nightclub had numerous young pretty girls wearing clothing that didn't leave much to one's imagination. Up until now, I hadn't seen girls dressed like that, except in girly magazines. Now, here they were in the flesh, begging for my attention. I was to learn this would be the scenario outside every overseas American military base.

Oh my, what was I to do?

Up until now, I still hadn't been with a woman. The navy had shown us videos of what could happen to a man's penis if he didn't wear protection. The pictures weren't a pretty sight. With that in the back of my mind, I didn't muster up the courage to fall for the temptation, so I left town still a virgin. Another time, another place.

Keep in mind, I'm a slow poke.

The next morning, I hurried to the dock to witness the arrival of my new home. I got there just in time to see her slowly floating into the bay.

WOW! Was she big!

I stood there in awe as I watched tugs maneuver her toward the dock. The flight deck looked to be at least a hundred feet above the waterline and as long as a football field. My new home happened to be one of the oldest aircraft carriers in the American fleet, but it sure looked brand new to me.

"Request permission to come aboard," I proudly said, saluting the officer on duty.

"Welcome aboard, sailor."

This would be my home for the next three and a half years.

I was very excited to begin this new adventure, but my first night onboard was to be a nightmare.

All new personnel were assigned the bottom of three stacked bunks in a tightly confined compartment. A sailor worked his way up through seniority. I had just crashed in my bottom bunk that first night when the rest of my shipmates began returning from shore leave. They were noisy and mostly drunk. Just as things finally quieted down and the snoring began, the guy above me leaned over and puked all over me.

Yea. Welcome aboard.

The ship was a floating city with a crew of three thousand men (no females back in those days). Meals were served twenty hours a day. Protecting America was a round the clock operation. We worked in twelve-hour shifts. It was hard work with very little play.

On August 4, 1962, during my second cruise, Marilyn Monroe was found dead in her bedroom. Marilyn had earned the film industry's title of *Screen Sex Queen*. She was the favorite pinup girl of most servicemen, including yours truly. I had her picture taped inside my locker door. The one where she is standing over the air vent on the streets of New York that blows her skirt up. So naturally I was devastated. You will discover later why I mention this now. It has to do with the name 'Monroe'.

In the meantime, life went on as usual aboard the ship.

There were always battle station drills, but in November of 1963 we had our first battle station announcement that was not a drill. We were in the middle of the Pacific Ocean and wouldn't you know it, I was right in the middle of a shower.

WHOOP WHOOP! Man your battle stations. This is not a drill!

We each had only a few minutes to get to our assigned stations before all watertight doors were locked down. I grabbed my pants and took off like a bat out of hell.

This could only mean we were at war. We would spend a few tense days on edge, before we were told to stand down. Only then did we learn about the shot heard around the world, President Kennedy's assassination.

During my tour of duty, I would visit Hawaii, Japan, Hong Kong, the Philippines, and Okinawa. The ship's home port was in Alameda, California.

Every ship and naval base had a baseball team. You know my love for the game, so I tried out for the ship's team. I would become the regular shortstop, as we played the base team in every port we visited. I found out I could be really good in almost every sport I played. What a difference from my younger days!

So, why the difference?
I suspect the entities keeping watch over me knew.

LIKE A VIRGIN

> *I made it through the wilderness, somehow I made it*
> *through. Didn't know how lost I was until I found you…Like*
> *a virgin, touched for the very first time…*—Madonna

Bet you had been wondering if and when I'd be losing my cherry. It took awhile, but I finally got acquainted with the birds and the bees!

During my navy stint, I visited many places and met many women from various cultures. In Japan, I visited Kobe, Yokosuka, Yokohama, Tokyo, and Hiroshima. Yokohama was the place where I finally lost my virginity. We passed through Yokohama as the ship was heading back to our home base in Alameda, California, shortly after I had boarded the ship in Subic Bay.

Seagoing sailors had havoc-wreaked love lives. We were never in one port long enough to establish any kind of a meaningful relationship. We had enough time ashore only to get drunk and to get laid. The native girls knew this and willingly provided their hospitality—for a few Yen, of course.

In a Yokohama nightclub, I ran across one such girl. *Konnichiwa! (Hello)*, she said.

I don't recall her name, but she was a Japanese Geisha, schooled in the art of pleasing a man. She also was willing to teach me how a man can please a woman. I figured that if I was new at something, I might as well learn from a pro. She spoke no English, but communication proved to be no problem.

She taught me well. I was never to be shy around or afraid of the opposite sex again. She taught me a rather simple technique: *look the girl in the eye, smile, and say hello!* Now why hadn't I thought of that?

I was so fascinated with her teachings, in fact, that I lost track of time. In foreign ports our liberty expired at midnight. The sun shining through the bedroom window brought me to my senses.

The ship was scheduled to leave port at nine that morning. To make matters worse, there were Japanese anti-American protesters outside the base, making it difficult for me to get back on base. I eventually pushed and shoved my way through the angry protesters and scampered onboard a split second before the gangplank lifted.

Of course, I was determined to be AWOL, and put on report. It was my first offense, so I got off lightly, with just a restriction to ship at the next port. The next port just happened to be Hawaii. Fortunately, this won't be the last time we were to visit Hawaii.

SOS

This time please someone come and rescue me…
S.O.S. please somebody help me.— Rihanna

I spent many nights on the carrier flight deck, gazing at the vast array of stars. There were millions of them. In the middle of the ocean they were especially bright and appeared close enough to catch. Many nights, the shooting stars would put on a breathtaking and amazing performance. Their exhibit left me thinking that there had to be other life forms in such a cosmic universe. I dreamed of hitching a ride on a starship.

Step aside, Captain Kirk, it's my turn to travel and explore new worlds and civilizations.

On my third and last Far East cruise, I thought I might get that chance. I was on deck one night, doing my routine star gazing, when I saw something that looked familiar. I can't really explain why it seemed so familiar, it just did.

Almost immediately, I felt a slight tingling sensation cloak my body, as the hair on my arms came to life and began to dance about.

It was the same sensation I had experienced that night on the country road outside Clinton, just before the freak accident.

In the night sky, I quickly noticed the same type of blinking lights, in the same formation, appear about ten miles away, on the horizon. A beam of light suddenly shot from the lights in the sky and moved downward toward the ocean surface. Then the beam disappeared as suddenly as it had appeared. In a flash, the three lights rose in the sky and vanished into the universe.

The hair on my arms returned to normal and the tingling sensation stopped. I can't explain how, but somehow I suspected what might have happened.

"Radioman Hay, report to the radio room on the double," I heard over the ship's intercom.

I had the Con (duty) that night and had just taken a break. I could feel the excitement in the radio room as soon as I stepped through the door.

"We just received an S.O.S.," shouted the excited radioman who had been monitoring the emergency band.

A ship was in danger. It turned out to be a Russian trawler. American fleets were always shadowed by these suspicious fishing boats. They were constantly snooping and spying on U.S. fleets. We knew who they were and what they were doing, and they knew we knew. It was a cat and mouse game, since we couldn't do anything about it in international waters.

International law required us to respond to an S.O.S., so we took advantage of the opportunity to board their vessel. No U.S. personnel had had that opportunity in the past, so our boarding party was very excited to be able to board a Russian spy boat. Everyone's adrenaline was flowing faster than a class five whitewater rapid.

It definitely wasn't a fishing vessel, as we had suspected all along, even though everything about it looked fishy. We couldn't find one fish onboard, let alone a fishing pole. There was however, a lot of fishy electronic equipment, enough that we wondered how the boat could stay afloat.

The Russian crew was completely disoriented. They appeared to be in shock and looked scared shitless. Only one of them spoke. He babbled in broken English, about some strange-looking flying machine, with small hairless creatures hitting them with a beaming light and a crewman gone missing. Nothing he said was making any sense to anyone in our boarding party, except maybe me. I suspected I might know what they had experienced. Something in the back of my mind told me I had been there and done that. However, I felt it best to keep my mouth shut.

We could smell Vodka on their breath, so it was assumed that they had to be drunk. What happened to the ship and its crew was later classified top secret, so if I were to tell you the rest of this story, I'd have to kill you. That might not be good for future book sales. I can say it was another one of those big government cover-ups that you don't hear or read about in the news.

This incident enforced my thoughts that human beings weren't the only living creatures in the universe after all. But my thoughts didn't last long as we were thrown into a war.

Shortly thereafter, the *Hancock* became involved in the Vietnam War. For forty-five days at a time we would be on station off the coast of Vietnam, bombing night and day. We would put to port in Subic Bay for three days of R&R (rest and relaxation) and then return for another forty-five days of bombing. I'll never understand how such a small country took such a pounding and still won the war.

Another case in point, one of our slow prop aircraft fighters, used for low-level bombing, landed with an arrow stuck in its wing. This had us shaking our heads in disbelief. Just who was this enemy, anyway? Shooting a crossbow at an airplane? Unbelievable!

WHOOP WHOOP, man your battle stations. This is not a drill.

The North Vietnamese finally decided to test our air defenses. We picked up a fleet of PT boats and a few MIG aircraft on our radar, heading right towards us. Lucky for them they veered off, just before we were prepared to blast them to hell. A U.S. naval fleet had enough firepower to destroy anything that threatened it, except maybe an alien spacecraft.

So why did we lose that war? I'm just a sailor. Ask the politicians. They're the same ones running the country now.

Back in the States, hippies were making love, smoking pot, and protesting the war. They would burn their draft cards and the American flag, while we were fighting and dying to protect the liberties they were protesting. They called us war-mongers and baby killers. We called them a bunch of draft dodging momma pussy boy cowards, who didn't have the guts to defend the liberties they were protesting.

The Vietnam vet was the only veteran who was spat upon and cursed for serving his country. We dared not wear our uniforms while on leave. No one was thanking us for our service to country. Shame on you citizens for treating us that way. It was a bitter pill to swallow and left a bad taste in the mouth of all Vietnam veterans, as you can tell by the tone of my voice. That was a sad page in American history.

Hey, hippies, it was the politician, not the soldier, who screwed that war up.

Those who served their country knew it was the soldier, who salutes the flag, who serves beneath the flag, and whose coffin was draped by the flag, that allowed the protester to burn the flag.

WHY DO FOOLS FALL IN LOVE?

Why does my heart skip this crazy beat?…
Why do fools fall in love? —Joni Mitchell

"Hey, G.I. Joe, you want girlfriend? My name is Dolly," said the most gorgeous doll I had ever laid eyes on! Her contagious smile and electric bedroom eyes lit up both me and the bar room! She was a bombshell and a brick house, wrapped in one enticing package!

"Well...Hello Dolly. My name is Tom. Heaven must be missing an angel," I said, as I looked her in the eye and smiled back.

I was on my third and last Far East cruise when I met Dolly. The ship was in the Philippines and I was on liberty, in search of a good time, just running my game. Love was the furthest emotion from my mind.

By now, I had no problem relating to women. I had had many opportunities to practice the Japanese geisha's teachings.

But Dolly really rang my bell. Of course it might have had something to do with her see-through blouse and painted on jeans. All heads turned cause she was a dream. She said I was a tiger she wanted to tame. No more love on the run.

How could I not surrender to her charms and discover 'love at first sight', from the condition of the condition I was in?

The long stretches at sea might have been taking a toll on my sensibility. Forty-five days at sea, attacking North Vietnam night and day, would wear a Marvel superhero down. Especially with only three days' liberty (always in Subic Bay, Philippines) and right back out for another forty-five days. This went on nonstop for six months.

Every time the ship would come to port, Dolly would be on the dock, waiting to comfort my weary body and soul. I often wondered how she knew when the ship was coming to port. All naval operations were supposed to be top secret.

On the ship's last visit before returning to the States, she told me she was pregnant with my child. Of course, being the fine gentleman that I am, I wanted to do the proper thing and marry her.

The ship's captain had to approve all marriages to foreigners, so I requested a hearing with him. During the hearing, the captain pointed out some facts that my *blind love* may have kept me from seeing. He informed me that it was common for foreign girls to want to marry a U.S. sailor. It was a free ticket to the States for them.

"Oh, no sir!" I said.

"Not my Dolly. She is different."

The captain rolled his eyes and strongly suggested I take her to a doctor, to confirm the pregnancy.

Well I'll be darned, she wasn't pregnant after all. During the examination, the doctor also discovered something else she had failed to mention. She had the clap (gonorrhea).

Now how in the world can the clap be mistook for being pregnant?

I set sail a bit wiser about the facts of life and with my manhood dripping, leaving Dolly to search for another lonely sailor to take her to America. Who could blame her for trying? Certainly not a naive and weary sailor.

SOUTH OF THE BORDER

The mission bells told me that I mustn't stay, south of the border, down Mexico way. -Willie Nelson

Remember my buddy Frank? He and I had signed up on the buddy program and spent boot camp together. After boot camp he went to store's clerk school. After that he was stationed at this tiny navy base in Southern California. The base was on top of a mountain, out in the middle of nowhere, just a few miles from the Mexican border. Frank never got to be a real sailor, as he never stepped foot on a ship during his entire four year enlistment.

We had kept in touch, so after my second cruise, I went to visit him while on leave. We decided to take some R and R in Tijuana. We almost didn't come back.

Frank had purchased a switchblade knife while shopping for souvenirs. He was waving it back and forth in front of my face, showing me how it worked. A Mexican cop observed his actions and must had thought Frank was threatening me.

The cop started shouting at us, as he drew his gun, and came running toward us. He was shouting something in Spanish, so we had no idea what he was so excited about.

The navy had warned all sailors who traveled to Mexico about their jail conditions. It was a place you didn't want to be in. With this in mind, Frank and I took off running for the border, which was only a few blocks away.

The cop saw us fleeing and started shooting. We heard the gunshots and put the pedal to the medal. About a block from the border I felt a sharp sting to my left pinkie. When I looked to see what had caused it, I noticed it was hanging by only the skin from the second joint.

Can you believe it? The stupid cop shot me!

Luckily, we made it across the border without further damage. I was able to get the finger repaired at a local hospital. They could only fuse the second joint, so that I could make a fist. The pinkie will never be straight again.

SHOULD I STAY OR SHOULD I GO

> *So come on and let me know. This indecision's bugging me…Should I stay or should I go?* —Clash

My, my, how time flies. I must have had fun. My four year navy tour of duty had expired. They tried enticing me to reenlist by offering a $3,500 bonus, a lot of money in 1965. On top of the money, I was offered shore duty in Japan, every sailor's dream tour.

How could I refuse?

It's been said that the navy is more than a job, it is an adventure. Well, it was time to give up the adventure and get a job.

Leaving the navy was a little scary, because they had provided three squares a day, medical, dental, and a roof over my head for the past four years. It was a frightening thought to be on my own. I had traveled half the world and had made some great friends. I enjoyed being a Radioman and sailing the blue seas. I had served my country with honor and was proud to be an American.

I can't really explain why, but I turned them down. I had this nagging feeling there was something much more exciting awaiting somewhere over the rainbow. I was ready to seek my fame and fortune, even though I had no idea how I was going to achieve it.

Keep in mind, I was still unaware of the abduction and the abductor's plan.

I got my honorable discharge and became a civilian. Three and a half years onboard a ship made for a salty dog. I was so salty they had to pour me down the gangplank when I left the ship. After I departed, I slowly turned toward the ship and my shipmates and saluted them one last time. A little bitty tear let me down.

After the navy, I didn't use my Morse code skills again until more than ten years later. Nonetheless, I never forgot them. Once learned, it was like riding a bicycle, something you never forget. The Code was stuck in my subconscious forever. It would be several years before I finally discovered how and why I had developed this unique skill, and how I achieved some of my other enhanced abilities.

The Comeback Kid's intriguing and mysterious adventures had only just begun.

All the while the abductors patiently watched, abiding to their schedule.

CHAPTER FOUR

THE CONUNDRUM

ACHY BREAKY HEART

Don't tell my heart, my achy breaky heart, I just don't think he'll understand. —Billy Ray Cyrus

About three months before my enlistment expired, I met Sylvia. To be honest, she was actually the deciding factor in my decision to leave the navy.

She was from Switzerland, working as a nanny for a wealthy San Francisco family. She was basically a plain Jane, as far as looks, but she had a nice figure, an attractive smile, a bubbly personality, and a charming European accent. She had me the first time she smiled and said "hello, is it me you're looking for?"

It didn't take long before she wrapped me around her little finger.

She was six years older than I, a very independent woman, and much more mature than anyone I had ever met. She became my first real girlfriend and, of course, I fell for her like a child.

I had always thought I would return to Missouri after my enlistment. I found myself seeking a job in the Bay area in order to be with her. She was a dream that had come true, someone with whom I could envision spending the rest of my life with. Unfortunately for me, however, she saw our relationship totally different.

Six months into our relationship, she informed me that her visa had expired and she had to return to Switzerland. Now, here's the kicker. She wouldn't be coming back. It was sayounara and I won't be seeing you anymore, ever again. I was devastated, to say the least.

She had been gone only a few weeks before I realized that I couldn't live without her. It had to be *true love*. Surely she was missing me too. I quit my job, sold everything but my clothes, packed my bags, and took off after my heartthrob. It was a one-way ticket through the tunnel of love.

Stupid is as stupid does.

Hey, give me a break. I was in love.

When I arrived in Zurich, Switzerland, I called and told her I had come to fulfill our (my) dream. She was surprised and shocked that I had traveled there to proclaim such a thing. However, she agreed to meet with me, once I arrived in her hometown of Lucerne. This was in September and it was starting to get cold, but the weather wasn't nearly as cold as she would be toward me when I finally arrived.

In the nicest and most polite way possible, she basically told me that my dream was her nightmare, and I should head on back home.

Now how could that be?

She told me it would be in my best interest to forget her and hightail it back to the States. She confessed to be in love with a married man and to be his mistress. She had taken the nanny job in the States to reevaluate her feelings toward him, but discovered she couldn't shake her love for him. He was the real reason she had returned to Switzerland.

Now she tells me?

Man, rejection by my heart's desire and one true love was a hard pill to swallow.

My heart ached so much that I got sick to my stomach and puked all over her floor. That made the situation even more painful and embarrassing. I had a hard time keeping anything down for the next few days. Sometimes love don't feel like it should. My only option was to swallow my pride, tuck my tail between my legs, and start the long, lonely, and sad journey home.

You can tell the world you never was my girl.
You can burn my clothes when I'm gone
or you can tell your friends just what a fool I've been
and laugh and joke about me on the phone.
But don't tell my heart, my achy breaky heart
I just don't think he'll understand…

I travelled to Luxemburg by train, then caught a plane to Greenland, and flew on to New York City. I had just enough money left for a bus ticket to the heartland.

The Comeback Kid would be needing a remedy for his achy breaky heart.

Little did I know that the abductors had a cure in store for me.

KANSAS CITY

I'm going to Kansas City, Kansas City here I come. They got a crazy way of loving there and I'm gonna get me some. —Wilbert Harrison

When I arrived in Kansas City, brokenhearted and with no coins to speak of, it was my birth mom who would come to my aid. She and I had been exchanging letters during my navy stint. It turned out to be a great opportunity to get to know her and my half brother, from whom Dad had so adamantly shielded me in my youth. I found out that she was not such a bad person after all. But my brother was another story.

I stayed with birth mom and her husband until she arranged a job for me with TWA. Through a friend, she had also arranged a job for my brother Mike a few months earlier.

After talking with Mom and doing the math, I discovered that my brother had been born one month before my oldest sister Sandy. Dear ole Dad had one in the hangar at the same time as evil ole Mom. Apparently, what was good for the goose, wasn't good for the gander.

When Dad discovered that I was seeing my birth mother, he refused to speak to me, a stipulation that lasted until his first grandchild was born, two years later.

It didn't take long for me to call my birth mother *Mom*, even though I wasn't really comfortable saying it. I soon got to know her side of my family, a part of my family that I had never known existed before.

Mike and I were soon able to share an apartment together. He was thrilled to death to have a brother too, as he had been raised an only child.

At our age, the only thing on our minds was the pursuit of the opposite sex. We were at the age where a man's penis replaced and took over his brain. Mike and I were no different, so we spent a lot of time beating the bushes and chasing tail. But he did most of the scoring, as I may have been still hurting from Sylvia's rejection.

My brother was a bona fide Casanova. Girls were attracted to him like flies to honey. He had that Hollywood look and charm. All he ever had to do was say, "Hi, I'm Mike," and the girls would follow him anywhere. However, his main objective was not romance. It was adding another notch to his bedpost. I would witness a few heartbreaks. I never really understood why women would be attracted to a guy who would treat them in such a way. I may have been a little jealous because I didn't seem to possess his looks and charm. I had to work it. I usually ended up with his leftovers and provided a shoulder to cry on.

On September 8, 1966, "Star Trek," a new science fiction series, debuted on television. It lasted only three seasons, but later became a cult classic. I would become a Trekie and boldly go where no man had dared to go.

The abductors would see to that.

PRETTY WOMAN

> *Pretty woman, walking down the street. Pretty woman,*
> *the kind I'd like to meet.* —Roy Orbison

"You take the brunette, I'll take the blonde," I told my brother. After all, blonde's have more fun. Right?

This was one of those life changing decisions, which may have been planned, that would disturb, perplex, haunt, and taunt me for the rest of my life.

Mike and I were attending a dance at the Wyandotte County Center in November 1966. I didn't really want to go that evening, but he talked me into it. I was still smarting from Sylvia's rejection, so I wasn't in a very good mood. But when I laid eyes on the green-eyed blonde, all my past heartaches suddenly disappeared and my mood changed in the blink of an eye.

I looked into her eyes, smiled, melted, and somehow uttered a *hello.* If I'd known my world was about to be turned upside down, I would have chosen differently that evening. Or, more appropriately, I would have turned around and ran as fast and as far away as I could.

Claudia seemed to be the perfect girl for a man ready to get hitched, as I was a prime candidate. She was so pretty, a talented artist, and a virgin to boot. She expressed a desire to spread her wings and escape the parental nest. I had traveled half the globe, sown my wild oats, and was ready to settle down and start a family. She was just what a doctor—or maybe an abductor—would prescribe for our situation.

Claudia made it clear, right from the start, that she was saving her virginity for marriage. We, or I should say I, found it difficult to be in a platonic relationship. So, after dating for only three months, I was hot to trot. I convinced her to elope to Oklahoma to get married. Nowata, Oklahoma, was the place for quickie marriages. Things are about to get very interesting.

While searching for the courthouse, I was directed by an invisible and taunted force to keep driving around. We ended up on an abandoned country road. I could sense something in the air, as I started having that tingling and hair-raising sensation again, just like I had experienced twice before.

Come on, man, what gives? I just wanted to get to the courthouse on time.

I know I should have turned around immediately and gotten the hell out of there, but for some reason I couldn't initiate the turn. It wasn't in their plan.

We soon came upon a herd of cattle grazing in a field. As we approached, they suddenly stopped grazing and stared in the same direction.

Claudia shouted, "Stop the car; we have to find out what the cows are looking at!"

"Okay," I said, "but you stay in the car."

All I could see was an enormous cornfield. It was close to dusk, and the glare from the sun made it hard to see anything in that direction. I put my hand over my eyes and squinted.

Then suddenly, a shallow figure materialized right out of the corn stalks. My first thought was that a scarecrow was on the loose. I was in a sleepwalking stupor as an invisible force propelled me toward the figure. A beam of light from the shadowy being, which was holding a gold-colored medallion, hit me in the chest. I was paralyzed but conscious as it walked up to me and measured my cranium. (Years later I would discover that I had been measured for a special type of helmet). The mysterious being then implanted another memory block and vanished with the sunset.

The next thing I knew I was standing alone in the darkening cornfield, not knowing how or why I had gotten there. The cows all stared at me like I was an alien invader.

When I returned to the car, my fiancé was sound asleep. She didn't recall or see a thing, since I had gotten out of the car. Several years later she would reveal to me what had happened to her that day:

> *I fell asleep in the car and had a most peculiar astral projection. I was out of my body and rising high above the trees. I looked to the sky and from the south approached a churning, rolling, gray wind. From the north came black rolling clouds with a beam of light in the middle. They were coming together over my head with tremendous speed. I assumed my body would be hit by the lightning that was created. The instant I became afraid, my astral spirit started to descend back into the car as I watched the ground and trees grow larger. I then felt warmth in my spinal area.*

All of this, however, was unknown to us that evening. I got back in the car, and somehow we found the courthouse, tied the knot, and returned to Kansas City. We made it home, and lived happily ever after.

Dream on, Tom.

Sadly, it would not be a story book happy ending.

Also, unbeknown to us was a news article printed the next day in the local Tulsa newspaper. The paper reported that a farmer had discovered crop circles in his corn field a couple miles south of Nowata.

In June that same year, Claudia and I went on a belated honeymoon. We flew to Los Angeles and rented a car to drive up Highway 1, which ran along the coast towards San Francisco. Claudia was five months pregnant.

We stopped in Carmel and got a motel room close to the monastery grounds. Right away, I began to feel the tingling again. I tried to convince Claudia we should leave. However, she seemed to be in a trance.

The boutique town of Carmel was set on gently rising bluffs above a sculpted rocky coastline. It was known for its neat rows of quaint shops and miniature homes. The place also had a thick air of pretention, and was peppered with tacky middle-brow galleries and mock Tudor tearooms.

There were no street addresses, there was no mail delivery, and there were no franchise businesses in town. Three small museums in the Mission Basilica, built in 1771, traced the history of the area and revealed the darker side of the dainty building with the graves of more than three thousand local Indians buried in the cemetery. It was somewhere in this area that Claudia experienced another encounter.

This is what she told me a few years later: *As we walked toward the monastery grounds, along the beach, I became very tired. It was dusk. Somehow we were suddenly on the grounds, while standing outside one of the monastery buildings, where I was attacked by a flock of wild geese. As they flew away over the ocean, our unborn went with them in spirit. I was upset and cried as we returned to the motel.*

She continued to say: *That night they abducted only me; you were left in the motel room. They took me back to the monastery. I was put on a table in one of the buildings. I couldn't make out who or what they were. I screamed as they cut open my uterus and our unborn was suspended in the air as they examined her.* (At this time we did not know the sex of the child she was carrying*). They must have installed another memory block, because my next memory was the next morning. While taking a shower I noticed a brown zipper scar from my navel down. It disappeared in a few days.*

The next day we went on a twenty-five-mile drive through an exclusive neighborhood.(I remembered going on the drive, but none of the things she was relating to me). *As we approached a gated community guard gate, you became very nervous. Your actions made no sense.* (As if any of this does). *It was as if you knew something would go wrong in there. You even screamed at me that you didn't want to go in there.* (I didn't want to go in but something urged me on).

The guard at the gate must have heard you, because he asked if everything was alright. It seemed strange to me that the guard would be wearing a military-type uniform.

Bizarre things started happening as we drove through the community. Flowers sprouted out of nowhere and lined the road as we passed. It was like a fourth-dimension manifestation; no other explanation could suffice. I was in awe, but you, Tom, were still terrified by something.

As we approached the beach area, flowers were still sprouting, almost down to the ocean. We departed the car and walked to a platform, which appeared to be some kind of a lookout. You were then attacked by a small being with blonde hair and wearing a one piece metallic cloth outfit. Somehow, we both became paralyzed. The being probed and poked various instruments into our bodies. Perhaps you remember what was done to you. (I didn't).

Rolling black clouds started to develop, emitting an intense laser-like light. All the flowers instantly disappeared. The whole area around us was stripped grey and bare. The being installed our memory blocks and sent us on our way. That's all I remember, except that for the rest of the trip and our marriage, you were never the same. I saw them before we were married too.

Years later, even after I discovered how to melt the memory blocks, I had no recollection of anything she had related here.

We returned to Kansas City and settled into a customary married life. In October, we became the proud parents of our first born daughter. Everyone commented how unusually large her eyes were.

A year and a half later, a historical event occurred. Apollo 11 lifted off on July 16, 1969, nine days after our son was born.

THE EAGLE HAS LANDED!

On July 20, 1969, President Richard Nixon and most of the world sat glued to their TV sets. America had beaten the Russians to the moon.

"That's one small step for man; one giant leap for mankind," said Neil Armstrong. Ever wonder if he might have seen any other footprints?

Lost in the excitement was the fact that the lunar module had landed with only thirty seconds of fuel left.

HOUSTON…WE HAVE A PROBLEM.

People of Earth were again glued to their TV sets on April 14, 1970, a day before my twenty-seventh birthday. The message came from Apollo 13, NASA's third Apollo mission intended to land on the Moon.

A mid-mission oxygen tank ruptured and severely damaged the spacecraft, forcing the crew to abort the lunar landing. The crew shut down the command module and used the lunar module as a lifeboat to make it safely back to Earth.

HEARTBREAK HOTEL

Well, since my baby left me, I found a new place to dwell. It's down at the end of lonely street, at Heartbreak Hotel. —Elvis Presley

My life was on cruise control and was what I had dreamed married life was supposed to be. Claudia and I had the perfect family, a girl and a boy, good jobs and lots of friends.

What could possibly go wrong?

Then suddenly, four years into our marriage, my little paradise hit a major bump in the road and I had another crash landing.

"I can't live like this anymore," Claudia told me, out of the blue. "We need to get a divorce."

Her words felt like someone had punched me in the stomach, as my breath and reality was knocked right out of me.

Claudia explained that she was becoming emotionally distressed and confused. She claimed to have had an out of body experience during which her spirit told her that she could no longer be in a sexual relationship, or in other words, she could not be a wife. I suspected that there had to be more to this than she was willing to reveal. Usually in these type of situations, there was a third party involved. Little did I know who that third party would be. Nothing either of us would ever suspect.

Where did all this suddenly come from?

At the time, neither of us had any idea what was happening. Whatever it was, it came on almost overnight. Suddenly, my perfect paradise crumbled and I found myself divorced. Claudia packed up and moved to Virginia Beach with the kids. Her spirit told her that was where she had to be. Those days the woman always got custody of the children, so I was left with no other choice but to watch them go.

A few months after she had moved, she would tell me about the abductions. She had learned how to melt her instilled memory blocks by fasting and abstaining from sexual activity. Ironically, the Bible also states that fasting and abstaining clears the mind and cleanses the soul.

Once these memory blocks were removed, she discovered the abductions, the aliens, and the things that had been done to her. She even told me that I had been abducted, not once but twice.

I had no idea what she was talking about and didn't believe her. I just assumed she had a fertile imagination, like most alleged UFO abductees. At the time, I was concerned only with putting my life back together again.

Still, the question remained: *how was it that my brother and I attended the dance that night when Claudia and I met? And why, pray tell, did I pick the blonde and not the brunette? Was it fate? Or was it planned?*

Would the Kid be able to check out of the Heartbreak Hotel?

He wasn't aware of it yet, but his life was about to get even more complicated.

CHAPTER FIVE

THE BEWILDERMENT

THE WANDERER

I'm the type of guy who likes to roam around. I'm never in one place, I roam from town to town…Cause I'm a wanderer, yeah a wanderer. I roam around, around, around. —Dion

The first few months after my divorce, I was a mess. I was a confused lost soul, drowning in misery. I just couldn't understand how my perfect world could dissolve so quickly. The more I thought about it, the more puzzling it became.

It was at this time that my brother Mike would put a bug in my ear that helped get me out of my rut. He had transferred in his job with TWA and had moved to the San Francisco Bay area. So, in February 1972, I transferred in my job and moved back to my old navy stomping grounds.

I heard the calling, Go West, young man, there's gold (as in blondes) in them there California hills. You would have thought by now I had learned to keep my distance from the blondes.

I found no gold. I had a hard time fitting into the hippy social environment. It appeared all everyone wanted to do was smoke dope and make love. Not that I'm against those things, but surely, there must be more to life. I felt like an alien on a strange and distance planet.

Carmel was just up the road from the Bay area. Something kept nagging me to return there. So, one weekend I decided to drive over and visit the old honeymoon grounds. I should have stayed in the Bay area.

As soon as I entered the city limits, I felt the tingling sensation creep over my entire body. Not only was the hair on my arms dancing, but memories from the last trip invaded my mind. Memories that I could never discern that still taunted me.

I made a quick U-turn, put the pedal to the metal, and shot out of town like a bat out of hell. That would be my last visit to that place, but soon another vacation spot beckoned. One that would be a lot friendlier and more entertaining.

"There's seven women to every man," spouted the number-one hound dog, my brother Mike, one day after suffering another boring weekend. Mike sensed I needed something to get my mojo back.

With those odds, Australia proved to be the perfect vacation spot for two red-blooded Americans on the prowl. So off to the outback we ventured.

What a long flight. It seemed to take forever to get there. When we finally arrived, though, the seven-to-one odds met us at the first establishment we walked into. There were females galore. They were pumped, lathered, and hot to trot. Talk about perfect timing.

It had been ladies' night, and male strippers had just finished performing. We got there just as the place opened to the public. We got the pick of the litter and had a fantastic dream vacation that definitely helped me crawl out of my rut.

On April 8, 1974, hammering Hank Aaron hit career home run number 715, breaking Babe Ruth's all-time home run record. As you can see, I am still following my favorite game.

In August of 1974, I again transferred in my job, this time moving to Jeddah, Saudi Arabia, the land of enchantment. Once more, it was Mike who inspired the relocation. He had transferred there a few months earlier, and it didn't take much to convince me to leave California, because the local social environment was driving me crazy.

TWA had a contract with Saudi Airlines and provided staff to train Saudi employees in the operation of their airline. This would be my task in the avionics field.

I received a 10 percent salary raise, free furnished housing, and utilities, and didn't have to pay any federal or state taxes on any of my earnings. What a deal! I would be able to save a lot of money. I planned to work there for five years and then return to my previous job in San Francisco with a nice portfolio.

Unbeknownst to me, my plans would go astray. Yep. It's those darn abductors again. They had other plans. I wish they would get on the stick and clue me in on them.

ARABIAN NIGHTS

> *Oh I come from a land, from a faraway place, where the caravan camels roam. Where it's flat and immense and the heat is intense, it's barbaric, but hey, it's home.* —Aladdin

ALLAHU AKBAR!
I came up out of bed like my pants were on fire.
What the Hell?
I had just fallen asleep. The cranky old noisy A/C window unit had kept me awake most of the night.

At the crack of dawn, someone shouted through a loud speaker right outside my hotel window. This call to prayer would happen throughout the country, five times a day, every day.

I had arrived in Jeddah, Saudi Arabia, around 10 P.M. the night before. There were no Jet ways, so the airplane parked on the ramp to deplane. As I departed, my breath was sucked right out of me. It felt like I had walked into an oven set at 350 degrees. It would not have taken long and I'd have been baked to a crisp.

Welcome to the land of enchantment.

Although I had visited many foreign countries, this would be the first time I lived in one. I was in for another cultural shock, but also for the time of my life!

The Kingdom of Saudi Arabia was the largest state in the Middle East by land area. Most of the land was desert and deserted. The country was founded by Abdul-Aziz bin Saud in 1932. The government had been an Islamic monarchy since the country's inception. Saudi Arabia had the world's largest oil reserves and was the world's largest oil exporter, thanks to American oil companies. Because of the oil revenue, every Saudi citizen was provided free health care and education. They paid no taxes.

The Saudi government was their religion. Their laws came from the Quran. Even the Royal family had to adhere to the law of the *Mutawa* (bearded religious police). They patrolled the streets with long sticks, ready to beat anyone not praying at prayer time or any women not properly dressed.

Saudi women could show no skin in public, especially on their face. They wore a face veil called a "niqab", which covers the lower half of her face, only revealing her eyes.

They had to be accompanied by at least one male relative and had to walk behind that relative. They were not allowed in the front seat of a car. They were stoned for adultery. Not an ideal environment for a liberal Western female.

Western males could mingle with Saudi males, but Saudi females were strictly off limits. We could be kicked out of the country just for looking at one. Apparently we were thought to be a bad influence on them.

The Saudi males were the bosses (at least outside the home), even though their native dress was a skirt. They could marry four wives at a time. The men could marry women of any nationality, but the Saudi women were allowed to marry only Saudi men.

If a Saudi female were to marry outside her nationality, she would disgrace and humiliate her family. Her father or brothers then had the right to execute her spouse and send her into a Bedouin tribe as a slave. It was a culture where the men had total control over their women, outside the home.

When a Saudi family had guests for dinner, the men ate first. The women got the leftovers, but only after the guests had departed. Most meals consisted of rice, vegetables, chicken, and lamb. They never ate meat from a pig. Saudis didn't use silverware and served their meals in plates, placed on a blanket on the floor. They ate with their right hand, never the left hand. It was considered unclean to eat with the hand that wiped your butt. It was a quick way to get excused from the meal.

What's a lefty to do?

When sitting on the floor to eat, they are careful not to point the soles of their feet at another person, as this is considered a grave insult.

I was invited for dinner by a Saudi co-worker one evening. I heard giggling from a back room and turned to see several females peeking around the hallway corner. My co-worker told me they were curious to see a Western male.

Sometimes at the city market I would catch a few Saudi women checking me out. I could see their faces through the thin veils that the younger generation wore. They would look me straight in the eye, smile, and sometimes wink, but none dared to speak.

I learned to say "Hello. You are very beautiful," in Arabic. That had them smiling even more, as they batted their flirting eyes at me. Very tempting, but I had been warned not to pursue the flirtations.

You'd best heed the warning, Tom.

The land of enchantment was the land of swift justice. Alcohol was forbidden, but accessible. Some foreigners had stills in their houses. Thieves had their right hand cut off for stealing. This would mean that they could never eat in public again. Murderers were publicly beheaded. I witnessed a beheading once. Not a pretty sight.

One of their most used phrases is "Inshallah," which means, "if it is God's will." For anything to be accomplished, it had to be "Inshallah." At times that would be very frustrating for Westerns, as it would take forever to get anything accomplished.

There wasn't much for foreigners to do in our spare time. The Saudis had TV, but there was only one channel and it was in Arabic. Once a week, a movie would be shown at the TWA compound. Most foreigners were provided living quarters bunched together in villas or apartments, surrounded by ten foot concrete walls owned by their employers.

The Red Sea provided most of our entertainment. Many of us rented small cabins on the beach and spent our weekends there. The Saudi weekend was Friday and Saturday.

We would snorkel, spear fish, and dive along the reef, which dropped to over a hundred feet below the surface about fifty feet from the shoreline.

Mike and I were diving one day, facing each other as we were taught to do. All of a sudden, about fifty feet down, I saw his eyes open real wide, as a look of fear appeared on his face. He started making gurgling sounds, as bubbles spouted from his mouthpiece. Frightened, I turned to see what had gotten him so upset. A big fish tail whipped past, and the current in its wake knocked us off balance. The great white shark vanished as quickly as it had appeared. The only reason I lived to tell you this was because it must not have been hungry that day.

MACHO MAN

Every man wants to be a macho macho man. To have the kind of body, always in demand. I've got to be a…Macho Man —Village People

My love life was taking a major hit. After four months I was wondering why in the world I would want to subject myself to celibacy.

Thank God for Ramadan! Heaven opened its pearly gates. I was about to get back in the saddle again.

Once a year, Muslims from all over the world flew into Saudi Arabia to visit Mecca, their holy city. Saudi Arabian Airlines would contract with other airlines to help with the mass number of Muslims coming into the country. The foreign airlines had lots of flight attendants, who had to lay over for a few days. In those days, flight attendants were female, young, cute, and mostly single. My salvation!

They stayed in hotels with armed guards to keep away undesirable critters, but where there's a will there will always be a way. I met Tina, Sharon, and Brenda at their hotel pool area.

Tina and Sharon were two chicks of color who were from the Bronx. We were of complete opposite cultures, even though we were all Americans. I was just happy to be around and chat in my native language with the opposite sex.

Now what would two Bronx babes want with a small town Midwest redneck white country boy with a southern slang?

We shall see.

Their last evening in the country, they were able to sneak me into their room. Oh my! I had never been with a black woman in all my travels. Neither had I been with two women at the same time. Even with the air conditioner set on high, the room got very hot that night.

First, they teased me by allowing me to watch as they made out. I'd experienced this in my dreams, but never before witnessed it in the flesh. It was an enormous turn on! But that was just their foreplay, as they then beckoned me to join them.

What an adventure I had, as they had their way with me, all night long. They did things to me that would have embarrassed my Japanese geisha girl. I'm sure you would like to hear more of the details. Sorry, but according to my editor I must maintain a PG-13 rating.

By morning, I was one exhausted but satisfied tomcat. They left Jeddah the next day and I never saw them again, but that night's memories will linger on.

Brenda was a cute English flight attendant who flew for British Airways. I met her a couple days after I had recovered from the Bronx girls episode. I was attracted to her English accent. She reminded me of Sylvia, a little bit. She wasn't able to sneak me into her room, but when she left, she gave me her phone number and invited me to visit her in England.

I would eventually take her up on her offer, but that is a story for another time. First my brother and I traveled to Egypt.

ON THE ROAD AGAIN

Just can't wait to get on the road again…Goin' places that I've never been. Seein' things that I may never see again. —Willie Nelson

I had been reading a lot in my spare time and came across an article on the pyramids of Egypt. I had a yearning to investigate their mysteries. I talked my brother into going with me.

For more than forty centuries, the skyline of the Nile Valley has been dominated by the mountains of pyramids. Intended as eternal monuments to the god kings of Egypt and as everlasting sanctuaries for their bodies, the pyramids, like the Sphinx, retain their enigma. Yet how did the ancient Egyptians raise such majestic structures without the wheel? Why did they build on such a superhuman scale? Can royal vanity alone explain the feat? Or is there some other secret motive still buried beneath the desert? The more they are studied, the more mysterious they become.

When we arrived at the pyramids, you guessed it, I started having that tingling sensation again. Yet this time it was very mild, compared to the others. No hair stood up and danced about. Nonetheless, I started to wonder if maybe this was a coincidence or if there was a solid correlation to these tingling sensations. I wasn't able to uncover it on that trip.

A couple months later the airline sent me to Miami, Florida, for L1011 autopilot training. After the training was completed, I figured I might as well take Brenda up on her offer. Remember Brenda? The cute British Airways flight attendant I had met in Jeddah.

She met me at Heathrow Airport and insisted I stay with her. I had no problem with that. Sleeping alone was not on my agenda.

I rented a car that had the steering wheel on the wrong side.

(*BEEP BEEP! Hey Yank, get on the other side of the road!*).

I thought they were going the wrong way. DUH! Turned out to be the bloody Yank.

Brenda was thrilled to show me around England. It's not a very big country. We attended the theater in famous Piccadilly Square, visited Hyde Park, and went to the beach. She introduced me to tea and Yorkshire pudding. Afternoon tea was actually a full meal. I was expecting a cup of tea.

We cruised the countryside and suddenly, in one particular area, I started getting nervous, because I felt that tingling sensation arise again. It was just a slight feeling, like I had had at the pyramids, not nearly as strong as I had felt in the Oklahoma cornfield or in Carmel's monastery grounds.

We were at a place called Stonehenge, located in a field two hours' drive west of London. There's no mistaking the huddle of ancient shapes that emerged suddenly on the horizon.

An air of mystery broods over Stonehenge, located in the English county of Wiltshire. It is one of the most famous sites in the world, composed of earthworks surrounding a circular setting of large stones believed to have been erected around 2500 BC. It was built by a culture that left no written records. Theories of the site's purpose include use as an astronomical observatory or as a religious site. It's still a mystery where the stones came from and how and why they were erected.

Learned men from all fields of science, as well as spiritualists, clairvoyants, and cranks, have studied the site to try to uncover the secrets of its past. Who built it, over four thousand years ago? Was it a temple of the sun? A royal palace? A magic shrine? An observatory for studying the heavens? Could it be a gigantic computer built centuries before the Greeks mastered mathematics? And why was I feeling a connection to this place?

In 1975, visitors were allowed to walk among the stones and even touch them. As I touched one stone, I had an immediate reaction that was impossible to describe. My mind seemed to turn inside out. Strange flashbacks sprung from my subconscious. Flashbacks that made no sense. I withdrew my hand from the stone and felt normal again, except for the hair on my arms doing an abbreviated two step.

"What's the matter, Tom?" Brenda asked. "You look like you have seen a ghost."

"We should go," I replied.

I dared not touch another stone.

A few years after our visit, Stonehenge visitors were no longer allowed to touch the stones. The reason given was because of serious erosion problems. Erosion? I don't think so. Come on man, Stonehenge had existed over 4,000 years and suddenly there are erosion problems?

One day, perhaps, will the answers to all of these questions be known? Or will these colossal stones guard their secrets forever? Their secrets were safe that day, anyway, because I left there with no answers and feeling like a lost soul in an unknown world.

As I write this story, there have been many UFO sightings over Stonehenge. One has to wonder, could there be a few alien ghosts wandering the grounds at Stonehenge?

After a few days with Brenda, I started getting antsy. I could tell we weren't very compatible. She was a prude and boring in bed, to put it nicely. Way too conservative for me. I hit a brick wall any time I would suggest something besides the missionary position, under the covers. To put it in proper perspective, she just wasn't my cup of tea.

For an excuse to move on, I told her I had to get back to work, even though I still had a few days of vacation left. She didn't seem to mind as I said good-bye.

Another one of those decisions that would have a huge impact on my future. But then hindsight never informed me that this was in the Abductor's plan.

POISON IVY

> *I just got back from the doctor. He told me that I had a*
> *problem…I tried to scratch away the issue.*—Jonas Brothers

I still had a few days before I had to report back to work in Jeddah, so I headed to the Heathrow Hilton Hotel discotheque lounge. The disco lounge was a great place to relax, meet interesting people from all over the world, and let your hair down. Most American Saudi Airline personnel travelling to and from the States hung out there on their layover. Never in my wildest dreams could I have imagined who I would meet there that night.

Sure enough, as soon as I walked into the lounge, I spotted a familiar face. It was Susan, a Saudi flight attendant and wife of a pilot who lived in the same apartment building as I in Jeddah. She was there with another flight attendant, both on their way to the States for a vacation.

As we sat there visiting, a couple Arabic men came over and asked the girls to dance. The girls turned them down, since they weren't really there to meet anyone. Arabic men are embarrassed to take *no* for an answer, so they kept coming back. I had heard that their attitude is that all foreign women are easy scores. The girls got a little irate with them and left.

Sitting there alone, I noticed that the Arabic men had come from a booth where they were sitting with three very attractive Arabic women. The more I focused on the women, the more I noticed that all three were absolutely glorious. Especially the one sitting on the end. There seemed to be a spotlight shinning on her.

She looked my way and our eyes locked. She had electric eyes that I could not ignore. She gave me a flirtatious smile that enticed my mojo. She swayed to the sexy and provocative beat of the disco music that was playing, all the while keeping her mysterious and sparkling eyes locked onto mine. She projected the thought that I was a tiger she wanted to tame.

Why weren't the Arabic guys dancing with these Arabian princess's, I wondered.

Okay, I thought, *two can play this game.*

The beat of Donna Summer's "Hot Stuff" inspired me to seek some adventure. After all, I was in search of a good time. Why not let her pet me?

So I promenaded over to their booth and greeted the lovely lady who had been giving me the eye.

"Assalam Alaikum," I said.

"Wa alaikum el salaam," she replied, with a pleasant, but somewhat shocked look on her face.

"Do you speak English?" I asked.

"Of course," she said, in a British accent.

"Would you like to dance?"

"I'd love to," she replied, to my surprise.

She didn't know it at the time, but she had me at "of course." I was a little stunned that she had accepted my offer.

As I escorted her out on the dance floor, my eyes had a hard time staying in their sockets. She was one beautiful, sexy woman! Petite with a model's figure. Dressed in a very tight and revealing evening gown. She looked to be all dolled up for the prom. I got a whiff of her perfume and it did to me what it was advertised to do. I was totally mesmerized.

As we danced, I could feel a vibrating electrical current keeping in step and dancing with us. We danced as one, as she was completely in tune with my rhythm.

"My name is Tom."

"I'm Fiza."

"Nice to meet you Fiza," I said, as I smiled and looked her straight in the eye.

"Nice to meet you too Tom," she replied.

"Where are you from?" I asked, to keep the conversation flowing.

"I'm from Saudi Arabia."

Holy Shit! Did she just say she was from Saudi Arabia?

"I'm going to school here in England. I came here tonight with my brothers and sisters," she replied.

All of a sudden, it felt like someone had pulled the plug or short-circuited our electrical connection. No wonder she had had that shocked look on her face when I greeted her. This juicy peach was forbidden fruit!

Oh-My-God. Common sense told me I had better escort her back to her booth. But, since when did I have any common sense, especially when it came to beautiful women and forbidden fruit?

I had figured that she was of an Arabic culture, but I had no idea that she would be from Saudi. If you have been paying attention, you would know this is a culture that keeps its women on a short leash. I'd heard stories, however, that Saudi women liked to let their hair down when outside their country. The disco lounge was an ideal environment for doing just that. I was about to experience it firsthand.

She must have seen the shocked expression on my face, as she asked, "Is something wrong?"

After recovering from the shock, I gathered my thoughts and said, "My eyes are having a difficult time adjusting to your beauty."

That brought a big smile my way and started the current flowing again.

We talked and danced for what seemed an eternity. Time stood still. I was back in seventh heaven and on cloud nine.

"I'd better get back to my booth; I think my brothers are getting upset with me," she suddenly said, as she looked toward them.

To say they were upset would be putting it mildly. A Western male had touched and conversed with their forbidden fruit. Her brothers started scolding her in their native language as soon as we approached their booth. The glare from their evil eyes was a message for me to skedaddle.

I got their meaning and high-tailed it to the bathroom outside the lounge. I figured that was the end of that wonderful encounter with an Arabian princess.

Darn, she was such a beauty!

When I came out of the bathroom, there stood Fiza. I felt my face lite up like a firecracker and my blood pressure spiked as she handed me a slip of paper and whispered in my ear, "Please call me in the morning."

She then turned and walked back into the disco, leaving me in a trance. I could only stare at the phone number in my sweaty palm as I slowly made my way to my hotel room.

Is this for real?

I tossed and turned all night. Could not sleep a wink. I thought morning would never come. I had never before gotten this hot and bothered over someone. Whoa, baby! I was on fire! Or was I playing with fire?

Oh, hell, Tom. Will you stop rationalizing? Just go for it. What have you got to lose, except maybe your nuts or maybe even your life.

I was adventurous, but I wasn't faster than a speeding bullet. Still, what the heck, it would be an exciting way to go! I was feeling invincible!

Ok, time to get some sleep.

I tried counting sheep. I twiddled my thumbs. I tried meditating. Nothing worked. I was still wide awake when the sun peaked through the window. Finally, it was time to dial the number she gave me.

Shit, what if she wrote it down wrong? Jesus! Would you stop thinking and just dial the number.

Okay.

I was shaking like a leaf, as I dialed the number. Didn't know if it was from excitement, or fear. I could hear in my head one of the songs we had danced to the night before: *Disco Inferno, burn, baby, burn.*

The anticipation was nerve wracking.

Ring-ring. Ring-ring.

"Marhaban" (hello), a male voice answered.

Shit, what am I going to say?

My heart was beating a mile a minute.

May I speak with the doll who knocked my socks off last night?" I wanted to say. Luckily, reality set in.

"May I speak with Fiza?" I said, in as high pitched a voice as I could muster.

"Hold on," he said.

All right! I pulled it off.

"Hello," said a female voice.

"Fiza?"

"Yes, who is this?"

It's that handsome devil you met last night at the disco, I thought to say.

"It's Tom. We met at the disco last night."

"Oh! Hi, Tom. I was wondering if you would call."

Wondering if I would call? Jesus! If only she knew what she had put me through all night long.

During our conversation, she told me she would be taking the bus that afternoon to Cheltenham, where she was attending school. It was a small college town about eighty miles outside London. It was a perfect opening.

"No need to take the bus. I have a rented car and would gladly take you," I said. "It would give me a chance to see more of the English countryside."

And maybe see more of that beautiful body, too.

After what seemed an eternity, but in reality was only a couple seconds, she replied, "Okay, that would be nice."

"YES!" I shouted, as I pumped my fist for a high five.

She told me where I could pick her up, and we ended our conversation. After I hung up, it suddenly dawned on me: *Am I walking into a trap?*

There was only one way to find out. No guts, no glory!

She had told me to pick her up at a certain location inside Hyde Park. I circled the area a couple of times to see if anyone was with her or maybe hiding close by. I was still fearful I might be falling in a trap. Remember, this peach was forbidden fruit that I was trying to pick. My adrenaline defiantly provided a rush and the will to give it a shot.

I finally decided she was alone and pulled up beside her. She was looking just as beautiful as she had the night before. She wore a simple white blouse and painted-on jeans. Her happy smile, electric brown eyes, and seductive perfume erased all my doubts. I could sense she was pleased to see me as well.

During the drive to Cheltenham, we talked a mile a minute. She told me she was studying for an architecture degree and had been living in England for a couple of years. There were no architectural colleges for women in Saudi Arabia, so she had convinced her father to send her to England to further her education. Apparently, she had daddy wrapped around her little finger. She wasn't letting her culture prevent her from fulfilling her dream.

Her father had four wives, like most Arabic men. He had gotten wealthy building apartment complexes in Jeddah. It was a small world, and I explained that I was now working and living there. What a coincidence!

I could sense her adventurous spirit. She told me that my boldness in asking her to dance, plus my baby blue eyes, left a grand impression on her.

The more we talked, the more I became infatuated with her. We defiantly had a spontaneous connection. Amazing how two individuals from completely different cultures could click the way we did. I realized she was indeed a unique woman and that maybe I had just found a real live story book princess.

She lived at the school dorm on campus, so I checked into a hotel room. She planned on showing me around town for the last two days of my vacation. I never did get to see the town on that trip, because we never made it out of the hotel room.

ALL NIGHT LONG

Well, my friends, the time has come to raise the roof and have some fun. Lose yourself in wild romance… feel good…all night long.—Lionel Richie

Actually, it became a two day and two night romantic marathon. As soon as I laid my suitcase down in the hotel room, we fell into an embrace. No matter how hard we tried, we just couldn't seem to get close enough to each other. There was no letting go.

Her touch made me as hard as a rock and set my body on fire. I thought I knew hot, but this heat reached a crucial boiling point in the blink of an eye. Our chemistry was explosive as fireworks at a fourth of July celebration.

We couldn't get out of our clothes fast enough. They went flying in every direction, as we ripped each other bare. In a heartbeat, we were naked as jaybirds as we dove onto the bed.

The force of our love making soon knocked us onto the floor. We scratched and clawed like two wild animals in heat.

We made love in every imaginable position we could think of and then some. When we attempted a pause to eat and bathe, they too became part of our activities. Passion cloaked and soaked our bodies and absorbed our souls.

I can't continue describing our out of this world mating ritual. It's that PG-13 rating thing again. I can say that we became one body, one mind, one heart, and one soul. We learned everything there was to know of each other, both emotionally and sexually. We became soul mates, as our hearts beat as one. We fell, head over heels in love.

After two incredible exhausting days that I will cherish for the rest for my life, we had no other choice but to finally come to our senses and snap back to reality. She had classes to attend and I had to return to work in Jeddah.

Actually, it was a blessing in disguise, because I don't think either of us could have physically survived another day at the pace we had set. It was exceptionally difficult to part, but we both knew I'd be back and that this was only the beginning to something very special.

We exchanged steamy love letters over the next few months. She would tease me by dabbing her perfume on her letters. It was agonizing to smell but not to be able to see and touch her. Needless to say, her letters had me climbing a wall. She was contiguously on my mind.

I had to keep quiet about her, even though I felt the urge to shout to the world that I had found my princess and soul mate. I was able to share my glory only with my brother Mike. Of course, he warned that playing with fire could cause severe burns, but my body and soul were already burning. No amount of water or common sense could douse the fire that burned within.

About a month later, I was playing softball and hurt my left big toe while sliding into home plate. X-rays at the hospital revealed it was broken, but the x-ray also showed a small metal object implanted in the tip of my toe. What it was and how it could have gotten there had the doctor and I baffled. Since it didn't seem to be bothering me, he couldn't see any reason in removing it.

I would eventually discover the object to be a tracking device. I would also learn there are many abductees with tracking devices implanted within them. Years later, when the tracking device implanted in my toe finally was removed, careful analysis determined that the device was made from material substances not known to exist on this planet.

So who would these devices be known to, and who could be tracking me?

It wouldn't be long before all the Kid's questions would be answered.

DREAM LOVER

Where are you, with a love oh so true, and a
hand that I can hold.—Bobby Darin

That summer Fiza and I were missing each other so much that she decided to take a gamble. I wasn't eligible for any more vacation for several months. She was on summer break, and as much as she hated being back in her country, she decided to come see me.

This was a risky decision, because it would be very dangerous for us to be seen or caught together, but forbidden love hath no sagacity—or, more properly said, love hath no brains.

Fiza's father had divorced her mother and she was living alone in an apartment in Jeddah. She was tickled pink when Fiza told her she would be coming to visit for the summer.

When Fiza arrived, she told her mother about us. Well, even in other cultures, mothers are very protective, but also compassionate, about their daughter's feelings. I was surprised to learn that her mother was thrilled to meet me, but, of course, our relationship must be kept from her father and step-brothers.

I was excited, yet nervous as a flea on a dog, the first time I went to see Fiza and meet her mom. Fiza warned me not to knock on the door unless the hallway was clear. It was strictly forbidden for a man to visit a woman without a male relative present, and even more so if that man was a Westerner.

When I arrived at the apartment, I had to pee, really bad. It must had been the excitement and anticipation squeezing my bladder.

After checking to make sure the coast was clear, I knocked, praying I had the right apartment. The door open and Fiza grabbed and pulled me in.

It took all my strength not to jump her on the spot. Mommy dearest was standing right beside us.

They both noticed my anxiety, as I was twitching in my need to relieve myself. Fiza's mother spoke no English, so Fiza had to translate, as I explained my situation. I heard them giggling as I headed for the bathroom.

I had been there but fifteen minutes when a big bad wolf knocked on the door. Fiza quickly ushered me into a back bedroom, before she answered the door. She soon snuck in to tell me that one of her step-brothers had heard she was in town and had come by to visit. She told me to remain as quiet as a mouse and stay in the room, out of sight.

I was stuck in that room for four hours, thinking he would never leave. I had no cards to play solitaire. There was no TV. The reading material was all in Arabic, so I sat on the bed and just twiddled my thumbs. Luckily, I had just gone to the bathroom before he had arrived.

The only safe place Fiza and I could be alone would be at my apartment. The only way she could get there, without detection, was to dress like a male and come in a cab. Arabic males wore a thawb (an ankle-length garment) and a keffiyeh (headdress), so it was easy for her to appear to be a male.

That summer Fiza would spend the week days with her mom and the weekends with me. We had to stay in my apartment the whole time she was there. It was too dangerous to venture out.

We didn't lack for entertainment. We listened to music, talked each other's heads off, and played games. Our favorite game was strip poker. Since we never had on more than two or three articles of clothing, the game didn't last very long.

I can't even attempt to describe our love making. We fell even more deeply in love. I can't believe how crazy we were. I wouldn't be here today if we'd gotten caught.

Crazy little thing called love.

It just so happened, that summer a major international headline appeared in newspapers around the world, telling the story of a Saudi girl marrying a non-Saudi Muslim.

She had eloped to Lebanon and married a Lebanese man she had fallen in love with. When her father found out, he had them kidnapped and brought back to Saudi Arabia.

As soon as they stepped off the plane, the man was shot in the head and killed by the girl's father. It was his right, by Saudi law. He took his daughter to a Bedouin tribe and forced her to be a sex slave for the tribal leaders. There was a TV movie made from that incident.

At the end of summer, Fiza returned to school in England. Amazingly, we didn't get caught, or so we thought.

TAKE IT TO THE LIMIT

You know I've always been a dreamer. Spent my life running around... Can't seem to settle down...Take it to the limit one more time.—Eagles

"You'd better leave the country, ASAP!" A Saudi co-worker whispered to me a week later.

"They know about you and the girl."

"Who are they and what girl?" I innocently asked.

"The father and brothers of the Saudi girl you have been with," he scornfully said.

"Ah shit! Really?"

"Really. If I were you, I would be getting out of the country as quickly as possible. I could be in trouble just warning you," he said.

Fiza's father and stepbrothers had somehow discovered our little secret. They were fit to be tied. To say I was in a heap of trouble would be putting it mildly. We'd gotten caught after all.

I never did find out how, but I later suspected it might have been one of the cab drivers who figured Fiza was a female. I couldn't take the time to investigate, because the law of the land had me on the run. I had fought the law and the law was going to win if I didn't get boot scootin'.

I informed my American boss of my situation and he confirmed that if I valued my balls, I best be hauling ass. He wrote me up for a medical leave. I rushed home, packed a couple bags, and caught the next plane out.

Oh man! There went my chance to become a millionaire. I had no time to tell my brother or say good-bye to my friends. Mike would eventually find out from my boss and ship the rest of my belongings.

When I signed the contract with Saudi Airlines, TWA guaranteed my previous job would still be available after my Saudi contract expired. The timing of this dilemma was perfect, because my contract was due to expire in a couple of weeks anyway, so I headed back to San Francisco, though I would have preferred otherwise.

I laid over in England to contact Fiza about what had transpired. She hadn't heard anything from anyone, but we figured it wouldn't be long before Daddy called her home. Were we heading up a creek without a paddle?

What were we going to do?

Forbidden love would have us on the run.

Had the abductor's foresaw and had anything to do with this?

OOPS, I DID IT AGAIN

*I think I did it again. I made you believe we're
more than just friends.*—Britney Spears

"Come to America with me. We should be safe there," I said.

"Okay." She didn't hesitate with her answer.

We rushed to the U.S. Embassy in London to get her a visa. Turns out, they were not in such a hurry as we were.

I had no idea obtaining a visa for her would be so difficult and time consuming. We found out there would be at least a two-month wait, because of a background check on Fiza. Of course, we didn't have two months, but they had all the time in the world.

I could not convince them that a background check would be dangerous for her health since she was a Saudi citizen. They had no understanding of or sympathy for our situation. However, they did put a bug in our ear, that if she were my wife, a visa could be issued in a matter of hours.

We looked at each other, nodded in agreement, ran outside, both raising a hand, and shouted in stereo, "Taxi."

Get us to the church on time!

England was similar to Oklahoma in terms of the ease of obtaining a marriage license. In a couple of hours I was a married man again. There was no time for a honeymoon, as we rushed back to the embassy for her visa.

The next day we flew the polar route from London to San Francisco. Somewhere over the North Pole, we joined the elite Mile-High Club. Don't ask how, but where there is a will, there will always be a way! Except now days the club's member is very exclusive because of all the new airline securities.

We had made our escape!

There you go thinking again, Tom!

IT'S ONLY MAKE BELIEVE

My hopes, my dreams come true, my life I'd give for you…but it's only make believe.—Conway Twitty

I got my old job back, an Avionics' line mechanic, with TWA. I purchased a small house in Fremont, in a middle-class neighborhood.

Fiza enrolled in college. She was able to get her credits transferred from England. I even enrolled in a few classes myself.

She fell in love with America and its freedoms. I taught her how to drive a car and she got her driver's license.

We were happy, really enjoying our life together, even though we spent a lot of time looking over our shoulders. More than once we suspected someone of following or spying on us. This was especially true if he or she looked Arabic. Yet as far as we knew, no one in her family knew where she had disappeared to. She didn't even tell her mother.

During spring break we took a trip to Rio de Janeiro, Brazil, for our belated honeymoon. Rio was absolutely beautiful, with gorgeous scenery and beaches. Fiza especially enjoyed going topless on the beaches, following the example of almost all the girls there. It was something she had dreamed to do, so she was taking full advantage of her newfound liberties. In Saudi Arabia, she would have been flogged for showing any sights of skin. Of course, I didn't mind, even though the beach scenery was straining my eyes.

After we got back from Brazil, Claudia let the kids visit for a week. We spent most of the time in Kansas City, as I introduced my wife to my family. They had no idea of our situation and I wasn't about to tell them. We went to Worlds of Fun, where I discovered my love of roller coasters.

All things considered, Fiza and I were happy campers. Of course, inevitably, there's a bear who comes along and spoils the campsite. Our honeymoon and paradise were about to meet a very unexpected and devastating end.

THE END OF THE WORLD

Why does the sun go on shining? Why does the sea rush to shore?
Why do the birds go on singing? Why do the stars glow above?
Don't they know it's the end of the world? —Skeeter Davis

A month after returning from Kansas City, Fiza and I went to a restaurant in Fisherman's Wharf, to celebrate the first-year anniversary of our marriage. It had been a hunky dory year, despite the worries. We were happy, in love, and having a wonderful time together.

What could possibly go wrong?

During the drive there and during the meal, Fiza seemed upset and disturbed. She was definitely not herself. When I asked her if anything was wrong, she said she was just tired. We had spent most of the previous night making love.

Halfway through the meal, I could tell she was struggling with her emotions. I knew it wasn't that time of the month.

I finally confronted her, "What's wrong Bubbles?" (Bubbles was my nickname for her).

"I know something is bothering you."

She reached across the table to squeeze my hands. Tears started running down her cheeks. Her words were choked as she replied, "Tom-Tom, (her nickname for me), you have made me so happy. I love you so much."

"Honey, you know I love you too." I said.

I had no idea what she would say next. I could picture it wasn't going to be pleasant.

She started weeping, unable to control her emotions. I started having a very bad feeling about this situation.

She then excused herself to go to the ladies' room to powder her nose. I couldn't imagine why she was being so emotional. I'd never seen her this way before.

I never saw her again.

She never returned from the bathroom. She disappeared from my life forever.

What's taking her so long? I wondered.

I had finished eating and had been waiting for her to return. Just as I got up to go check on her, the waiter brought me our bill.

Inside was a note:

Tom, they found me. I have to go with them. They said not to pursue me or they will not only kill you but your children also. I will always love you. Fiza

"NO! Oh God, please no," I cried, as I rushed out of the restaurant looking for her.

She was nowhere in sight. This seemed impossible, but my gut told me that it was probable. I knew I'd never be able to find or see her again. My princess, soul mate, and wife had vanished. It dawned on me, she had been saying good-bye. It was our last supper.

At the time, I had assumed that Fiza had been abducted by her step-brothers. I couldn't go to the police. I couldn't report her as a missing person. I couldn't pursue and rescue her. I couldn't do anything. I was between a rock and a hard place.

Driving home that night across the Bay Bridge, I cried my eyes, heart, and soul out. The emotional pain was far greater than any physical pain I had ever suffered. How can love hurt so bad?

Why does my heart go on beating?

Why do these eyes of mine cry?

Don't they know it's the end of the world?

It ended when I lost your love.

The Bay Bridge is several miles long, connecting San Francisco and Oakland, with Treasure Island in the middle. I found no treasure that night. To this day, I will never know how I made it across that bridge. Not many did in my state of mind. It had to be by the grace of God.

To make matters worse, my car radio was playing the song that perfectly described my feelings:

Are you lonesome tonight? Do you miss me tonight? Are you sorry we drifted apart? Does your memory stray to a bright sunny day, when I kissed you and called you sweetheart? Do the chairs in your parlor seem empty and bare? Do you gaze at your doorstep and picture me there? Is your heart filled with pain, shall I come back again? Tell me dear, are you lonesome tonight?

To this day I still think of Fiza every time I hear that song. I think of her every time I think of love. I think of her every time I think how it could have been. She was a courageous woman, born before her time.

How was the Kid ever going to come back from the end of the world?

The abductors knew, because it was time for them to initiate their plan.

CHAPTER SIX

THE AWAKENING

TIME

*Ticking away the moments that make up a dull day. Fritter
and waste the hours in an offhand way. Kicking around on
a piece of ground in your home town. Waiting for someone
or something to show you the way.*—Pink Floyd

Sadness, depression, misery, and loneliness came calling, all
wrapped up in one big nasty package. I started drinking and smoking
pot every day after work. I would sit and watch TV all evening, drag
myself to bed, arise, and haul my ass to work. The days dragged by,
slowly but surely. There had to be a purpose in life, but I hadn't a
clue as to what it could be.

I hadn't long to drown in my misery. Unbeknown to me, it was
time for the abductors to implement their plan. I was about to discover

a whole new and different world. A world no one had ever suspected existed, except maybe in a science fiction tale.

A month into my desolation, there came a knocking on my door. It wasn't the Raven, nevermore.

I was sitting in my recliner on a Friday evening, doing my usual monotonous routine. I answered the door to encounter two NASA officials. I recognized the patches on their shirt sleeves. But that didn't make me any less skeptical to invite them in.

"Thomas Hay?" One asked, as both flashed their ID badges so fast I hadn't time to see their names.

What they wanted and revealed would change my life forever, and probably will change yours too. Nothing would ever be the same, not for me, and not for you either.

What in the world does NASA want with me? I wondered.

Hold your horses, Pilgrim! All the suspense built up to now is about to be revealed.

Every human being on earth was aware of NASA's Apollo Program, and specifically the lunar landings, which had been called the greatest technological achievement in history.

So why hadn't anyone questioned how, out of the clear blue, mankind started developing these types of technologies so quickly?

The Apollo Program had been established to beat the Russians in the race to land the first man on Earth's moon. The program had ended in 1975, three years before I received my visitors tonight.

Apollo 17 marked the last manned mission to the moon, according to official government records. Most people are not aware, however, that official government records reveal only what the federal government wants the public to know or believe. The government has a way of sometimes distorting facts from the truth.

Okay…So what has this got to do with these two NASA officials knocking on your door?

You're so impatient.

The two NASA officials explained that the government required my services for a classified top secret mission. Remember, while in the navy, I had been cleared for such information.

The *Mission Impossible* theme song started playing in my head.

I began to envision a thrilling, but dangerous assignment that would take me to the far corners of the earth. Maybe even allow me to rescue Fiza or other ladies in distress. Step aside Tom Cruise, Tom Hay was about to take over the mission.

Ok, Tom. Snap out of it. Get back to reality.

If you insist.

The NASA boys explained that the mission (should I accept it) would take only a few weeks and then I would be able to return to my current job and dull life. My cover story would be that the airline had sent me to Florida for autopilot instrument landing training. No one would suspect otherwise.

For this mission, I would receive $25,000 a year, tax free, for the rest of my life.

WOW! Did I just hit the Power Ball jackpot?

Hold your horses, there was a condition.

Wouldn't you know it?

There's always a catch when something appears too good to be true.

The "condition" was that I could not reveal the mission to anyone, so help me God.

Now, why didn't that surprise me?

If I did, then all payments would cease. I would likely die from a rare disease or an unfortunate accident. If the disease or accident didn't do the job, I would be put on the IRS black list, convicted of tax evasion, and spend the rest of my life behind bars or locked up in a nuthouse.

Shit! What could I possibly be getting myself into?

Maybe I needed to give this some more thought.

Supposedly, twenty-five grand a year would not raise any suspicions. It wouldn't change my lifestyle or get me laid. Still, a calculator confirmed that it would amount to over a million dollars in a normal lifespan, a nice little nest egg for the future. Plus, I would be a patriot and doing my country a great service. I could even envision a movie deal over the horizon.

You should know me by now. This was an offer I couldn't refuse. The Godfather would be proud! I just hope I wasn't biting off more than I could chew. Needless to say, I was curious as a tomcat. What could the U.S. government want with a little peon like me?

"So what's the mission?" I asked.

"Before we can reveal that, you must sign this contract," one of the NASA officials said.

The contract basically stated that I couldn't, then or ever, or under any circumstances, disclose what I would be doing. I was slightly disappointed that I wouldn't be changing my outfit in a phone booth or flying out of a bat cave. Looks like here would be no movie deal after all.

But that didn't keep me from signing on the dotted line. I figured, what the heck. I needed something to add some spunk to my life.

Count me in, the whole nine yards. I hoped I hadn't just fallen for some elaborate hoax.

"By the way," I said. "I didn't catch either of your names."

"You don't need to know," they said in stereo.

"Okay...Sorry I asked."

Red flags were waving, but I didn't play attention. Dollar signs and being a hero were blocking my vision.

I was immediately flown to the NASA headquarters in Cape Canaveral, Florida, on a government aircraft, no less. I still did not know just exactly what my mission was.

When the first artificial satellite of earth slipped across a backdrop of stars on October 4, 1957, it was heralded in the United States not as a triumph of science and technology, but a bold, startling challenge to America's ideological standing in the world community of nations.

The former Soviet Union's Sputnik 1 satellite sparked a U.S. response, motivating the U.S. Congress to hammer out in early 1958 the National Aeronautics and Space Act. Signed into law on July 29, the act transformed the existing National Advisory Committee for Aeronautics (NACA) into a U.S. civilian space enterprise. That enterprise was named the National Aeronautics and Space Administration (NASA).

On October 1, 1958, just short of a year after Sputnik 1 was cast into space, NASA officially began to blueprint the nation's space program. NASA was an investment in the country's future, an agency empowered with a vision to boldly expand frontiers in air and space, inspiring and serving America to benefit the quality of life here on Earth, as well as someday in space. NASA centers would eventually spread throughout the United States.

The Cape Canaveral center was crawling with security personnel. There was no chance that even a cockroach could enter the facility without being detected and setting off an alarm. The place was buzzing with activity and you could feel an aroma of excitement in the air.

The services NASA required from me turned out to be the Morse code skills I had acquired in the navy. If you recall, I had achieved a code speed far superior to that of anyone else on record. Apparently, that record still stood. It still hadn't dawned on me at this point to wonder how or why I had developed that skill.

After dusting off the rust, I was back up to speed in no time. I hadn't lost my touch. D-day had arrived. It was time to discover the mission, and along the way I would also discover why and how I had learned my Morse code skills.

Brace yourself, a revelation is about to be exposed.

Roger, copy that?

DO YOU WANT TO KNOW A SECRET

Listen, do you want to know a secret? Do you promise not to tell,
whoa, oh. Closer, let me whisper in your ear, say the words you
long to hear…Listen, do you want to know a secret?—The Beatles

Bravo, you say. It's about time! We are finally getting to the nitty gritty!

NASA was convinced I had the right stuff to join the rest of the mission team. They started their explanation of my mission by first admitting that the government had been covering up some UFO sightings and abductions.

Well…how about that. Why am I not surprised?

"You and your first wife were among the abducted," they confessed. (Keep in mind, that at this point I hadn't yet melted my memory blocks).

"You've got to be joshing me," I said. "This is what my mission is about—UFOs and abductions? Sci-Fi stuff?"

To be honest, I was not really shocked or surprised to hear this. I bet you have had some suspicions too, huh?

It turns out, Claudia had been right all along. I should have suspected it, but I suppose I just wasn't able to believe and face it before this point in time. I suppose I had too many other obstacles clogging my mind. I reckon that puts me in the same category as most skeptical people, which probably includes you too.

Well, surely most of you can understand my reservations. I bet you had them too. Maybe you still do. Or maybe you're thinking that you knew it all along. If so, you are a step ahead of me.

In the back of my mind, I still thought that perhaps this was a hoax or maybe there was a movie deal in the works and somehow I had been picked to be the star. Surely there had to be a logical explanation for all this. Maybe they thought that if I believed their story then that would make the movie more believable? As you can see, my mind is contemplating every conceivable configuration.

The NASA officials continued their explanation by telling me that I didn't remember the abductions, because the abductors had installed memory blocks. During my first abduction, my Morse code skills were instilled, along with a few other generic modifications. I suppose that could explain my increased IQ, improved hand-eye coordination and eyesight, and some other enhancements that I really don't need to talk about.

My new friends did not reveal why my ex-wife was abducted, or at least not until later. That information was available only on a need-to-know basis, and I didn't need to know just yet. I would be hearing those words quite often in the coming weeks.

The NASA officials never implied that extraterrestrials or aliens were the abductors. They did say that the abductors had been spying on us since "who knows when." Another need to know.

It was just after the Apollo Program when the abductors decided to make first contact, the NASA officials explained. Evidently, the abductors had learned enough about us and desired a talk. We had done something that frightened them.

I wondered what it was that brought it on. Maybe their comfort zone had been invaded? Maybe our technology was getting close to exposing them? I suppose there could be a hundred different reasons. I would eventually find out, and it wouldn't even be close to what I had imagined.

The abductors agreed to share some of their technology with us, as long as the government continued to deny their existence. This at least partially explained why our technology had developed so rapidly in the past few decades. If you would stop and think about it, our technology had advanced more in the last two decades than it had in the last 2000 years.

The NASA officials also said that the abductors had prepared some of those abducted (which included me) for when the first contact with us would become necessary. I would learn later, however, that there were other reasons for the abductions as well.

Many abductees were identified as NASA personnel, along with other VIP's.

After first contact, NASA established a top secret UFO department, known only to the American president and a few top U.S. military personnel. Of course, to this day, Uncle Sam still denies their existence. Knowledge about it was on a need-to-know basis, *AND YOU DON'T NEED TO KNOW.*

I was still having a hard time believing all this shit, but the dollar signs and possible movie deals kept tickling my curiosity.

NASA's story just kept getting better and better. They further explained that many abductees had been abducted several times. Some had to be prepared in stages, they said, since the human body and mind couldn't absorb a whole lot of stuff at once.

Now that makes sense, right? Because right then, I was finding all of this pretty hard to absorb. Probably, you are too. Bear with me.

The first abductees were prepared to help develop an effective communication device. It turned out that the abductors could see and hear, but had no verbal speech, therefore making communication with us painfully slow and nearly impossible, even with their technology. They communicated with one another using mental telepathy. Apparently, our brain wave patterns were different, so mental telepathy did not work with us. I would discover later that it was because humans were capable of using only about ten per cent of our brain at this stage of development.

So why couldn't the abductors speak? Well, apparently, developing telepathic communication caused them to lose their vocal cords. The old saying, *if you don't use it, you lose it,* hypothesis. I would find out later that this applied elsewhere, too. Think reproduction. But I am getting ahead of myself.

Since the abductors could not communicate with us verbally, communication was painstakingly slow. This was why they abducted and gave me and others skills that would help us to develop an effective communication device.

The abductors identified to the government a number of abductees whom they had programmed to develop and assemble such a device. The team consisted of mathematicians and musicians, along with electronic, sound, and lighting experts. Added to the team at the last minute was yours truly, as I was considered to be the Morse code guru.

OORAH!

Hey, not bad for a navy guy, huh?

Are you still with me or are you thinking I've gone completely nuts? Who in the world would believe this shit? I warned you at the beginning that your life, your existence, your reality, would never be the same.

Anyhow, at this point I figured that I might as well play along. My curiosity was overriding my common sense, compelling me to find out where this would lead. Besides, the nest egg, and the thought of rescuing distressed ladies, was still playing in the back of my mind.

Our team was put to work right away. In a few weeks' time, working around the clock, we were able to develop a fast and effective device to communicate with an intelligent being that had no vocal cords.

The device used light, sound, and music delivered by Morse code. Morse code is an international language. Apparently, it must be intergalactic as well. Although this last statement was just an assumption.

I swear, George Lucas and Stephen Spielberg must have been abductees too, because their movie two years later, *Close Encounters of the Third Kind*, featured a carbon copy of our device.

All of this, of course was leading up to my next encounter, which, this time wouldn't be a forced abduction. I would be going willingly.

Prepare yourself. This is what we all have been so anxiously awaiting.

The Kid was about to come face to face with the abductors.

CHAPTER SEVEN

THE PHENOMENON

Now that faster communications had been established, I soon discovered that the abductors had further plans for some abductees. My NASA buddies told me they required assistance in another project. Yours truly was number one on their list.

Turns out, I was the only one among the team members selected to participate. I had no idea why I was the only one chosen. However, I would eventually discover there would be others.

All communications with the abductors thus far had been conducted by government higher echelons. Keep in mind, at this point I still had not had any direct contact with the abductors, or at least none that I could remember. Nor had I had direct communications with government higher brass. I still had suspicions that someone could be pulling the wool over my eyes.

Then I received a statement from my bank, confirming my first payment. It was time to reevaluate. Maybe a little wool wasn't so bad if it made me a millionaire. Perhaps there was some truth to this after all.

I had no clue as to why, what, or where the next mission would be or take me. Strictly need to know. But curiosity got the best of the tomcat again and I agreed to go along. Although I had a feeling I would be going whether I wanted to or not. The two NASA officials who had first contacted me escorted me to another government aircraft.

Man, this must be costing the taxpayers big time.

The three of us boarded Air Force Two, and off we flew into the wild blue yonder. As you may know, Air Force Two is the Vice President's plane. So I was either a VIP, or a sheep being taken to slaughter. Either way, there was no turning back at this point.

The interior of the plane, which was equipped with a bar, lounge and private sleeping quarters, resembled a hotel suite more than it did a passenger airplane.

I sure did get the VIP treatment. I had my own cute flight attendant to wait on me hand and foot. The food and drinks were fit for a king. Check out the menu:

CAVIAR
TAMALE PIE

A baked tart filled with ground beef, corn meal, tomatoes, chili and spices, topped with melted cheddar cheese.

TOSSED GARDEN SALAD BOWL

An array of fresh, crisp, garden greens consisting of romaine and Boston lettuce, endive, red cabbage and shredded carrots. Tossed with an assortment of special garnishes and served in an individual "Taiwan" bowl. Choice of creamy California avocado or chef's Italian dressing.

ENTREE SELECTIONS
CHATEAUBRIAND

The Aristocrat of Roasts…A double Tenderloin of Beef, selected from Choice Midwestern steers. Cooked to your desire and carved at your table. Accompanied by Sauce Béarnaise, a stuffed baked potato and seasoned vegetables.

ALMOND PINEAPPLE PORK

A specialty from San Francisco's Chinatown, roasted Pork Loin slices, blended with Pineapple chunks, Snow Peas, Bamboo shoots, Water Chestnuts and Black Mushrooms and sprinkled with toasted Almonds. Served with Fried Rice.

DESSERT CART
GOLDEN GATE ICE CREAM SUNDAE

Fancy French vanilla ice cream topped with Golden Galliano sauce and sprinkled with chopped walnuts.

HOT APPLE PIE

Tangy apples baked in a flaky crust and served fresh from the oven with choice of rich vanilla ice cream or Cheddar whip.

I had the tamale pie, tossed salad, chateaubriand, and the hot apple pie. During the meal the flight attendant kept my wine glass filled with a Paul Masson Pinot Chardonnay. My after dinner drink was a Marina Coffee (Galliano, Kahlua, coffee and whipped Cream).

Needless to say, I was a spoiled brat in seventh heaven.

Stuffed to my eyelids, I crawled into my private sleeping quarters and immediately fell into a deep sleep.

I had no idea where we were going, although I suspected that my NASA buddies knew. It was a long plane ride over lots of ocean. When we arrived, I looked out a window and recognized the place immediately. We were landing on Easter Island.

I had read about Easter Island and its statues, and that's how I recognized the place. The island is called *the navel of the world* or *the eye turned towards the sky*. It was a place of surging breakers, precipitous cliffs, towering volcanoes, and open windswept slopes, all located on the most remote island in the Pacific Ocean. Dominating the landscape, of course, were the island's famous statues.

These massive, stylized figures, known as *Moai*, made of buff-colored volcanic stone, are both majestic and disturbing. Their heads are immense, their expressions are brooding and disdainful, their ears are grotesquely elongated, and their chins are jutting and powerful. Their arms hang rigidly alongside their legless trunks. Their hands extend stiffly across their protuberant bellies.

Could this be what the abductors looked like?

It wouldn't be long before I found out.

No one knows what these great Gulliver's were doing in this Lilliputian land, a mere forty-five square miles in extent. The statues seemed like sentinels, but over what were they standing guard?

We were met by several U.S. Army personnel as we deplaned. The army officer-in-charge seemed to know the two NASA officials, even though there were no introductions. They escorted us in army vehicles to a small rundown shack, located at the base of a gigantic volcano.

The one room shack was dusty, dirty and empty of furniture. Not even a stool to sit on or a pot to piss in, possibly a good thing, because the wood floor looked like it wouldn't support much weight. There was one small dirty window covered with a large spider web. They had no maid service here.

In the middle of the room was a trap door with an old leather strap screwed to it.

One of my companions grabbed the strap and lifted the trap door. The door squeaked as dust filled the air and made me cough.

"You first," he said, as he handed me a flashlight.

"Why me? I have no idea where to go."

I could imagine them closing the door behind me, trapping me in this God forsaken place.

"Just follow the stairs. We will be right behind you," said one of them.

I was somewhat relieved when they did follow.

The trap door opened to a stairway, which led to an elevator. Only my NASA buddies and I took the elevator.

Down we went, to who knew where. It seemed to be a bottomless pit, as it took forever to reach our destination.

"May I ask where we are going?" I said.

"No. You'll find out soon enough," responded one of my buddies.

For cryin' out loud, what was I getting myself into?

My anxiety level started to rise again as my mind started to imagine all kinds of scenarios. I could picture the abductor to be a flesh eating alien and I was to be its main course.

Just focus on the nest egg and the dames who may be in distress, Tom.

Roger, copy that.

We finally reached our destination and departed the elevator into a narrow, damp, and dimly lit passageway, where we were greeted by two men. Water dripped from condensation on the ceiling, making the passageway slippery.

"Watch your step," said one of the Secret Service agents.

I could tell who they were by the patches on their shirt sleeves. I knew these people were usually assigned to VIP government personnel.

They escorted us on a long cautious walk before we finally entered a large cavern. My eyes immediately focused on a large dome stationed in the middle of the room. It was about twenty feet high and maybe fifty feet around. It was filled with a thick swirling misty vapor, which made it difficult to see anything else that might be inside.

"What is this place?" I asked, not really expecting an answer.

"It's__"

"Need to know," interrupted one of the Secret Service guys.

"We can tell him, since he'll be getting a memory block after all this is through," responded the other agent.

Giving me a memory block? What in Sam Hill are they talking about?

"Yeah, you're probably right. Your NASA buddies will explain."

With that, the two Secret Service agents departed the cavern.

The two NASA officials looked at me, and then one said, "This is the abductors home base, and one of them wants to talk with you."

Now why didn't this news surprise me? I bet you have suspected this all along, huh?

"Yeah, okay, it's about time. Let's rock and roll," I said.

I was starting to feel my Wheaties. You know, the Breakfast of Champions. My adrenalin had me pumped and I felt like I could take on anyone or anything.

One of the officials handed me a bizarre-looking helmet and said, "Put this on."

"What is this for?" I asked.

This helmet, as it turned out, was why the abductors had measured my head during the abduction in Oklahoma, though at the time I had no idea that this had been done.

You do remember me telling you about this, right?

"It's to communicate with the abductor. The helmet is much faster than using the Morse Code procedure."

"Ok, so how does it work?"

"That's above your pay scale. Just put it on," he commanded.

The helmet looked and felt like leather. It resembled the helmets worn by football players back in the early days of the game. But this one had lots of tiny blinking lights flashing all different colors. I could feel a slight vibration and hear a slight eerie high pitched sound coming from it.

I reluctantly slipped it on. It conformed perfectly to the shape of my head. Suddenly, it became deafeningly quiet. Sort of like the calm before a storm.

I immediately observed a mysterious figure emerging from the swirling mist inside the dome. I had finally come face to face with an abductor.

Now, you may have been expecting some God awful creature, slobbering slimy sticky stuff, to spring forth and scare the shit out of us. I suppose I had too, but, thank God, this didn't happen. I hope you're not disappointed. I know I wasn't.

Heaven knows, I had no idea what I was looking at. In the not too distant future the being would be appearing countless times in movies, TV, and books, but at this particular moment in time, what I saw was totally strange and unfamiliar.

The abductor resembled Spielberg's *Close Encounters* aliens. I told you, Spielberg had to have been abducted too. How else could he have known what they looked like?

The being was humanoid, small in stature. Probably about five feet tall, but with a little more meat on its bones than Spielberg's aliens. I would say his (I'm assuming it was a he) weight was almost in proportion with his height. It had a pale grayish complexion. It's head was slightly oversized for the body. I saw no traces of hair, no eyebrow or eyelashes. Its face was dominated by large, lidless eyes above a small nose and mouth, and instead of ears, I could detect a small opening on each side of its head. It was clothed in a one piece gray metallic cloth of very fine texture.

Thank God it wasn't Sigourney Weaver's *Alien* creature. I can't imagine what I would have done if something had sprung from its mouth and screamed at me. Most likely died from fright or surely piss in my pants, right on the spot. I know there wouldn't be time to find a Johnny-on-the-spot.

Pray tell, the abductors really are aliens and this is what they look like?

It appears that way.

But, keep in mind that sometimes things are not what they might appear to be.

However, in this case, it appears aliens really do exist, but what are they doing here on our planet? Where have they been hiding? Where are they from?

When one stops to contemplate how vast the universe is, it is unreasonable to believe that humans could be the only life forms. Still, I wondered why these beings had chosen to come here and to make contact with me.

Maybe it was a situation similar to what Superman experienced. Perhaps their planet was being destroyed and they had to relocate. They had meandered around the galaxy, searching for a suitable home, and just happened to stumble upon our doorstep.

How long had they been visiting? Maybe now all the mysteries of the world, the Pyramids, Stonehenge, Easter Island, and numerous others, would be answered. Was mankind finally going to get an explanation?

All these questions swirled around in my head. I wondered if I was losing my mind. Was seeing really believing? Or was this a dream, a hallucination, or an elaborate hoax?

I stood there in shock and awe, gazing at this extraordinary being. Suddenly blocked memories started escaping from my subconscious. I saw what had really occurred on the country road outside Clinton. I saw what had actually happened in Oklahoma and Carmel. My mind was flooded with a vast collection of previously blocked memories.

These memories were coming faster than the speed of light, more quickly than I could comprehend.

The Comeback Kid was about to blow a fuse.

CHAPTER EIGHT

THE INSCRUTABLE

Stories of UFOs and abductions have been recorded throughout human history. Surrounding mankind on our planet are numerous unexplained sites. As we begin to question our past, often eager to find clues to the future, we increasingly realize that a wealth of civilizations have preceded us. Many discoveries have proven to be so extraordinary and so enigmatic that they pose more questions than answers.

We have uncovered fascinating evidence about much of our mysterious prehistory, yet so many mysteries remain. Who built the five cities of Tiahuanaco on the roof of the Andes? Why was Zimbabwe created, and by whom? What of the mysteries of Atlantis, the Bermuda Triangle, Roswell, crop circles, and countless other sites?

Could the answers to many of the world's mysteries be that in prehistoric and modern times aliens from other worlds have been visiting our planet? How could the evidence be denied? Do aliens really exist on Earth?

Here are just a few examples of numerous substantiations that have been recorded:

1561, Nuremberg, Germany

Descriptions exist of a battle in the sky lasting about an hour, which ended with a large crash outside the city.

October 24, 1886, Maracaibo, Venezuela

The U.S. consul reported a bright object, accompanied by a humming noise, that appeared over a hut. The occupants later displayed symptoms similar to radiation burns and poisoning. Several days later the trees surrounding the hut withered and died.

1947, Roswell, New Mexico

An FBI investigator, along with several other witnesses, reported that three flying saucers had crashed. Each saucer was occupied by three bodies of human shape, but with pale gray skin, with large eye sockets, and of only about four feet in height. They were dressed in metallic cloth of a very fine texture and of a type never before seen. The investigator was shipped off to another position across the country and told to keep quite.

June 1953, Falmouth, Massachusetts

A U.S. Air Force radar operator and pilot bailed out of their craft because of engine failure. They had reported they were in pursuit of a UFO. Plane and crew members were never seen again. Six months later, in Lake Superior, another U.S. Air Force pilot and his plane vanished while pursuing a UFO.

January, 1966, Wanaque Reservoir, New Jersey

A bright light in the sky led to traffic jams and overloaded police communications networks. The UFO shifted colors as it shot a beam of light towards ice near the dam. Among those who reported seeing the craft were Mayor Hagstrom, Chief of Police Elston, Captain Joe Sisco, Sergeant Thompson and Patrolmen Waster.

September 15, 1991, Space Shuttle *Discovery* (in orbit)

Video taken during the mission STS-48 shows a flash of light and several objects flying in controlled patterns. NASA explained them as ice particles. However, Dr. Jock Kosher proposed convincing arguments against them being ice particles.

September and October 2003, Pleasant Hill, Missouri

Some area residents saw a strange row of lights hovering over a field between Harrisonville and Pleasant Hill. The lights disappeared as suddenly as they had appeared. During the next few weeks, many area residents would spot these same type lights. Farmers soon found strange formations in their fields. This is just a few miles from the site of my first abduction.

October 2011, Kansas City, Missouri

Eighty-seven UFO sightings were reported in the Kansas City area, the most in the world for the month of October. This just happened to be the month before I published my memoirs. Coincidence?

Project Bluebook

A government study on UFOs from 1947 to 1969. A fourteen chapter report was issued, but chapter thirteen was missing. It still is to this day. What was in that chapter and why did it go missing?

These few examples are just a drop in the bucket. So why, despite the evidence, are most people still unable to accept or believe UFO sightings, aliens, and abductions? Credible witnesses, including airline and military pilots, astronauts, law enforcement officials, and other prominent figures, including a U.S. president (Jimmy Carter), have reported UFO sightings. There is credible evidence that President Eisenhower met with aliens.

Countless more have claimed to have been abducted by aliens. So, why do people think these claims are only fantasies, trickery, or overactive imaginations? Why can't folks believe what is happening right before their very eyes?

Is it because the U.S. government has brainwashed and convinced the public that UFOs, aliens, and abduction stories are just pranks? After all, they can't have people believing that stuff. Think about it: if these stories were known to be true, it could disrupt civilization as we know it. There could be panic in the streets. It would change the history and beliefs of mankind. That's why our government will forever deny UFOs and all alien existence.

Then there are those who throw another monkey wrench in the equation, aiding the government position with their tomfoolery.

Many UFOs are thought to be alien spaceships. The abductions are thought to be by extraterrestrial beings. However, Alpha Centauri, the next closest star system to Earth, is approximately twenty-five trillion miles away. Present-day spacecraft would take about 70,000 years to cover that distance. That's a long time to spend without a trip to McDonald's or a Wal-Mart.

Suppose the trip could be done in 2,500 years and the extraterrestrials had plenty of time on their hands. Their spacecraft would have to travel at a speed of a million miles per hour. That's a thousand times the speed of the fastest recorded modern aircraft. I bet even Superman or Star Trek's *Enterprise* couldn't achieve that speed. So the odds that another life form could travel that far are astronomical.

And then, there is the story of the Anunnaki. Approximately 450,000 years ago, Alalu, the deposed ruler of the Anunnaki on Nibiru, escaped his planet on a spaceship and found refuge on Earth. He discovered that Earth contained plenty of gold, which Nibiru needed to protect its diminishing atmosphere. They began to mine Earth's gold, and this caused many political battles for power.

Then, around 300,000 years ago, the Anunnaki decided to create a race of workers by genetically manipulating the primates of planet Earth. The result was Homo sapiens, human beings. Eventually, ruler-ship of the Earth was handed over to the humans and the Anunnaki left, but it is written that someday they will return. Could the Anunnaki be the abductors? Could the abductors be our God?

Those who believe and have reported that they have been abducted are a heterogeneous group, widely dispersed along demographic and cultural lines. These types of abductions are a rare phenomenon and have been estimated to have occurred to over three million people in America and countless others throughout the world.

There is a remarkably precise correspondence to their reports. Abductees exhibit relatively little psychopathology. Hypnosis has been used to confront, confirm, and allow others to experience their memories. However, hypnosis only allows the abductee to see through the memory blocks. It does not dissolve them. That is why after being revived from hypnosis, they still have no memory of the events.

Both subtle and highly robust physical evidence accompanies some abductions. Many abductees share some remarkably similar experiences.

Is it just a coincidence that in the last fifty years technological achievements have progressed more than in all previous years of history? And that between the years 1950-1970, UFO sightings and abductions skyrocketed. This alone, should make you wonder. The answer may be blowing in the wind and smack dab in front of our eyes, an answer that even a blind person could see. Or, an answer that may be buried deep within your own subconscious.

So what is it that keeps most people from believing in aliens and abductions? Has the government really done such a great job of brainwashing us? Are we skeptical because we have watched too many science fiction movies or read too many science fiction books? Are we that afraid of finding out the truth?

Well, hold onto your hat pilgrim, because you are about to get hit in the head with a startling revelation.

CHAPTER NINE

THE REVELATION

HELLO

Is it me you're looking for?...'Cause I wonder where you are and I wonder what you do. Are you somewhere feeling lonely?...Hello, is it me you're looking for?—Lionel Richie

Wait a minute. Wait just one frickin' minute. What's going on here? Someone has to be pulling my leg. BIG TIME. It's not like I was born yesterday, you know, I suddenly thought, while staring at the being in the dome.

Reality has to be around here, somewhere.

No one is pulling on your leg, Tom, I suddenly heard.

The words, clear as a bell, reverberated within my mind.

I am quite real and aware of when you were born, the words continued to form in my mind.

Suddenly, I'm hearing a voice in my head.

"What the hell!" I shouted.

You do not have to shout, or for that matter, you do not even have to speak. I can hear your thoughts as well as your voice, my mind said.

What's with this voice in my head?

I remembered reading that some abductees reported hearing voices in their heads. They were thought to be loco. Was I losing it, too?

The being standing inside the dome was looking straight at me. I never noticed any lip movement, but somehow I knew that was where the voice was coming from.

I looked back at whatever it was and thought, *Are you talking to me?*

Of course, Tom. The helmet enables us to communicate through our thoughts, I heard.

Okay, that's pretty cool, I thought.

The room temperature can be adjusted, if you are chilled.

"Oh, no. I'm fine. That was just a figure of speech," I said.

Whoops, I kept forgetting I didn't have to talk. This was going to take some getting used to, speaking without talking. I'd always heard that it was wise to think before talking. This would be a good time to put it to use.

Tom, let me introduce myself, I heard.

Yeah, please do! I thought.

I'd started to get the hang of not speaking. I was dying to know who the little guy was and where he came from. His answer will blow us away. It did me anyway.

I am Monroe Hay, number VI. I am your great-great-great-great-great grandson.

"What the...?" I said out loud.

It took me a moment to gather that thought, and when I did, I figured maybe there was something wrong with the helmet. This Monroe thing surely hadn't said what I had just thought I heard. I tapped on the helmet in case there was a bad connection.

Finally, all I could think to think was, *what did you say?*

My name is Monroe Hay, number VI. I am your great-great-great-great-great grandson.

That's what I thought I had heard. Apparently, there was nothing wrong with the helmet. Had to be a mental problem with this being.

Really. You don't say! You're my great-great-, uh, how many greats was that?

Think of it as five generations, Tom, came the response from the being calling itself Monroe and claiming to be kin.

"BULLSHIT! AND I'M PETER PAN. You expect me to believe this crap?" I shouted, to no one in particular.

I turned and looked at the two NASA officials and said, "You guys hearing this shit?"

They just stood there with blank looks on their faces.

My shout must have hurt Monroe's ears or mind or whatever, because I saw the abductor's face recoil and distort, as if he were in pain.

There is no reason to shout. I am unfamiliar with bullshit, Peter Pan, and crap, but I can assure you, there is nothing wrong with your hearing. At least not for a few more years, Monroe said.

I completely understand your skepticism, since your government has eviscerated our existence.

Are you still with me? I bet you're thinking what I'm thinking, huh? This can't be real! It's got be an elaborate hoax.

At this point I began to think that I must have had a brain fart, had blacked out, was hallucinating, or maybe had been dreaming, because I was pretty sure that I'd lost touch with reality.

I surveyed my surroundings, noting that I was still in the same room. I also noticed that the little being still stood there inside the dome. It didn't seem like it could be a dream, but I pinched myself just to be sure.

Okey Dokey, I felt the pain of the pinch.

I told myself to take a deep breath and calm what nerves I had left. I decided to play along with this masquerade and find out where it led.

I recognized the name Monroe as a family name, but I had a hard time seeing a family resemblance. The abductor's nose certainly wasn't anything similar to the Hay nose. It was looking more like Michael Jackson's surgical nose.

Okay, if what you say is true and we are related, let me think, now that would make me your great-great-great-great-great grandfather. Right?

Yes, Tom, you are correct. I will explain the nose at a more proper opportunity.

Christ, how did I get so frickin' old all of a sudden?

My thoughts were going a mile a minute and had left my mind in the dust. How could mankind's future generation be aliens and we be related? Not even someone from Arkansas could have achieved that feat. The maze was getting more complicated by the minute and I had a feeling I might be lost and never find a way back.

We are not aliens, Tom. We were born here on Earth. We are humans who have evolved to what you now see. We are mankind's future generation.

Yeah, right. Now that totally makes sense, humans who look like aliens, I jokingly thought.

I began to think that maybe I should take what money I had earned and excuse myself from this fiasco. This had gone on long enough. But Monroe interrupted my thoughts.

Let me explain further, he said.

Advanced human technology, in your future, conquered time travel. What you call UFOs have never been alien spacecraft visiting Earth, as most people suspect. The crafts we use for time travel are mistaken to be alien flying saucers. You have never had extraterrestrials visiting the Earth. That is mankind's most improbable myth. Extraterrestrials or so called aliens have been human descendants, traveling back in time.

Through the years, we experimented with human gene splicing. Genetic manipulation has caused humans to evolve to our current appearance. Your descendants are what you call the abductors.

Well, I'll be darned, I thought. *Now don't that beat all. Who would have ever thought?*

This puzzle was starting to come together. You got to admit, it does make some sense.

Besides my help with the communications device, what else could you want with me? I asked.

Don't get the wrong idea here. I still was not falling for all this science fiction crap. I figured I might as well keep playing along, though, and see where it led.

It is your brother, Monroe replied.

He requires your assistance.

My brother! Now why am I not surprised at that? I should have known he would have something to do with all this, I thought.

If you remember, my brother and I didn't really get to know one another until after high school. That's when we started running around together. I saw him step in a lot of shit, but somehow he always came out smelling like a rose.

He'd tell me, "You may have been *born ready,* Tom, but I was *born lucky.*"

Now I wondered what shit he had stepped into this time. Hopefully Fiza's family hadn't taken my punishment out on him. I worried that maybe his luck had expired and he might now be in dire straits.

The last I knew, he was doing quite well in Saudi Arabia, I told Monroe.

I am not referring to your brother Mike. I am talking about your other brother. He is called Tom-Tom.

My other brother? Called Tom-Tom?

Shit! The milkman must be involved after all. I never knew the milkman, but he seemed to be always coming around. He had to have been one brave SOB.

The only other explanation that I could think would be that this was a stunt for that new popular TV show, Candid Camera. So where was the Camera?

Tom-Tom? Now who in the heck might he be? I asked.

He is your clone, Monroe said. *That is why he is referred as a brother.*

"That's it," I said. "I've heard enough. I'm out of here."

As I turned to leave, however, the two NASA officials blocked my way.

"You might want to stick around and hear him out," one told me.

It seemed that I had no choice but to heed his advice.

This is so fracking nuts, I thought.

Do you require nutrition? I heard from Monroe.

Now why would he ask that?

No, I do not require nutrition.

I require some common sense that would make good sense. A good yoga class might come in handy about now.

Okay, just in case I'm not understanding you, I finally said, *you're saying that I have a cloned brother, whom you call Tom-Tom. Is this correct?*

That is correct, I heard.

How could this have happened? I asked.

We used your DNA and cloned you, Monroe explained.

He has now matured to your exact age and is an exact replica of you.

The abductions and Monroe the great grandkid I had started to believe, but now a clone? An exact replica?

Come on, man. That might be reaching for the stars a bit, don't you think? Last time I checked it wasn't April Fool's day or Halloween. All this has got to be some kind of a joke, I thought.

It is no joke, it is not April Fool's day, and I am certainly not wearing a Halloween costume," Monroe replied.

I kept forgetting that he could hear my thoughts. I realized that I needed to exercise a little more caution, because I sensed that he might be getting a little irritated with me.

Let us return to the subject, Tom. Unfortunately, cloning has not gone as planned, he continued.

Excuse me? Certainly it didn't have anything to do with me or my genes.

No, Tom. There was not anything wrong with your genes, except maybe your eyesight, but we fixed that, along with some other enhancements. Originally we had not planned to abduct you. You happened to be in the right place at the right time.

I'm thinking it was the wrong place at the wrong time.

So, it was you who caused my car wreck?

No Tom, you hit a pothole, remember? At least that is how you informed your father, Monroe quickly pointed out.

We happened to be in your neighborhood and witnessed your car spin out of control. We pulled you out just before the car went out of control. We knew you would survive the crash and it would have no effect on the time wrap. We have to be very careful not to disturb it, as it would change the future. It provided an opportune time to abduct you and do some research. We determined that you would be a good candidate to help develop the communications device. During your examination, we discovered your testosterone level to be very high. That is why we cloned you.

Well, thank you. Thank you very much, I said.

I have no idea why I would be thanking him. It seemed to be the proper thing to say.

From the look on his face, my Elvis impression went right over his head.

So, if I may ask, besides helping to devise the communications device, why then are you cloning people from your past? I asked.

Future generations wanted a perfect world where all human negative behavior could be eliminated. Imagine a world with no jealously, envy, war, pollution, crime, or disease. A world with one race and one creed.

We created our almost perfect world. Unfortunately, during the creation, we lost the ability to reproduce. To save mankind from extinction, we needed healthy reproductive glands. The only place to get them was in the past, Monroe said, with a sad look on his face.

That's what caused the blood in my semen? You stole my sperm?

I would not say stole, more like borrowed. You are quite capable of producing more.

This started to get interesting and maybe, just maybe, I had started to believe. How about you?

So why do you have to abduct so many people? I asked.

As you can see, I am really getting into it now.

Unfortunately, not all abductees are healthy or have good genes. We could not tell this until after an examination. The years between 1960 and now have proved to be mankind's healthiest span.

That could explain why abduction reports exploded during that era.

When did the cloning start? I asked.

I will explain everything in due time, he replied, *but for now, your brother requires your assistance and time is running short. I require you to come back to the future with me and help restore order.*

Did I hear that right? I wondered.

Had he just said he wanted to take me back to the future? To restore order?

Surely I'd be waking up from this dream world any minute now. Someone needs to POKE me on Facebook. But on second thought, let me be. This could turn into an amazing and intriguing adventure.

Move over Doc, Marty and Biff. It's time to fire up the flux capacitor.

The Kid was going ' back to the future'.

CHAPTER TEN

THE JOURNEY

One of my NASA buddies handed me something that resembled a surgical mask.

"You might want to put this on," he said.

"What's it for," I asked, "and please don't tell me it's another need to know."

"You'll find out soon enough, smart ass. Just put it on and don't remove it until you're told. You'll be wise to follow my advice. This is as far as we go. Have a nice trip," he sarcastically added.

Hey dude, why the sarcasm? Probably another need to know. Or, perhaps maybe he was a wee bit jealous? Never did get either of their names. I didn't know it at the time, but I would be seeing them again.

I noticed Monroe put a mask on too. I would discover later that our future siblings were susceptible to ancient smells and germs, especially from primitive kinfolk.

Hey, it wasn't my fault that I hadn't showered that day or the day before, and maybe even the day before that. Things had been moving so fast that hygiene was put on the back burner and the least of my concerns.

An entrance suddenly appeared in the dome and Monroe stepped out.

Please follow me, and watch where you step.

He led the way down a flight of narrow and steep slippery stairs that led to another room. There was condensation everywhere. The adjourning room was smaller than the cavern we had just left. It was filled with all types of lighted panels, flashing in every color imaginable as it emitted creepy sounds. It looked to be something right out of a scary Frankenstein movie.

Entering the room I got hit with a God awful odor. The same type smell Missouri gets when the west winds blow from Kansas. Yes, I could smell it through the mask.

Shit, I thought.

Are you required to relieve yourself? Monroe asked.

That may be a good idea, since it has been awhile and I have no idea when I may be near a john again, I replied.

Who might John be? He asked.

Just another ancient expression. A place to get relief can be called a john, a bathroom, a restroom, an outhouse, or a loo, among a few others and depending on which culture or time a person's from.

I suppose being of a future generation would make it difficult to understand so many different expressions having the same meaning. Maybe ole Monroe hadn't kept up on his English lessons, or idioms are no longer used in the future.

After visiting the *John*, (yes, I washed my hands, Mom) Monroe led the way down another narrow and dimly lighted passageway.

We emerged into a humongous room at the base of a volcano. As I looked up, I could see the night stars emerging through the opening at the top. Millions upon millions of stars lit up the night sky. I stood there in admiration of the astonishing display. It reminded me of the times I had spent on the USS *Hancock* flight deck in the middle of the ocean.

I looked around the vast room and saw another amazing sight. A flying saucer was parked in the middle of the room. That's really the only way I could describe it. It had to be as big as a football field. It was grayish in color and was suspended in the air about two feet from the ground. It had strobe lights at the top and at the bottom. An entryway was open and a walkway extended to the ground. There was a constant humming reverberation that tickled my ears. The size and sight of the ship put me in a trance.

Monroe snapped me back to reality when he explained that they had established an operations base at the bottom of the island's biggest volcano. Being from the future, they knew it would not erupt anytime in their time line. Easter Island was safe and secure, and was their only time entry base.

Their main time craft was called the mother ship. She carried smaller craft in compartments on her outside hull that were miniature versions of the mother ship. The smaller craft could also travel to different time quantum's and were mainly used to travel around the globe, once they had entered a conciliatory time quantum.

Most UFOs observed were probably the smaller craft. They always travelled in a tight formation of three. Why three? Need to know.

Got'cha!

Most abductees would be taken to the mother ship for their examinations and gene enhancements. Don't ask how, he didn't explain. Most likely, another need to know.

Monroe mentioned that I had been on the mother ship twice before. Of course, it wasn't by choice and I wasn't given a tour either time onboard.

As I passed through the mother ship entry door, Monroe directed me to a small room that resembled a shower. I was instructed to remove my mask, undress and step into the compartment.

A fine, sweet-smelling mist sprayed my body. He explained that the mist sanctified my primitive odors and germs. A one piece gray metallic cloth outfit, similar to the one Monroe was wearing, was waiting for me when I stepped from the shower.

We made our way to the cockpit (flight deck, to be politically correct). The room was round with two large flight chairs positioned on a small platform in the middle of the room. The ceiling and walls gave an optical illusion of blending together as one. The outer walls were covered with all sorts of flat screen monitors and panels flashing all sorts of colored lights. Beneath some of the panels were high back chairs that were secured to the floor. There were holograms stranded in mid air throughout the room. Gene Roddenberry must have been an abductee too.

There were several other type beings present, but Monroe didn't bother with introductions. Most likely they were not relatives.

Two were completely different than Monroe. Their human form more closely resembled our generation. They had perfectly proportional bodies. One that you would imagine an Olympic athlete to have. They had distinct features with unblemished olive complexions. Both were extra ordinarily graceful, beautiful and illustrated a gentle expression. They had mid length blond-white hair and deep blue sea eyes. Both stood well above Monroe. In fact, they were slightly taller than my six-foot frame. Both wore a one piece uniform that formed tightly to their body. Each carried what appeared to be a weapon strapped to their waist.

One was most definitely a female. I was hypnotized by her unique beauty and sexuality. She observed my stare and enchantment, and gave me a smile that radiated calmness, gentleness, and goodness. I could have been imagining it, but I could swear she gave me a wink to boot.

Monroe brought me back to reality when I heard his dissatisfied grunt. He was probably reading my exotic thoughts. I'm beginning to wonder if we have the same genes.

Genetically engineered warriors to enforce and protect social order, he explained.

Yeah, she could spank me, I thought.

That thought brought another grunt and throat clearing from my grandson.

I was to find out later that the genetic enhancements also made them highly sexual beings. I bet you can't wait to get to that part!

After I recovered from my trance, I continued to survey the flight deck. I noticed some of the panels were similar as those in the small room we had passed through at the base of the volcano. The writings and symbols on the panels were Greek to me. The biggest panel displayed two dates that I could identify. The first was that day's date and time. I hadn't realized it was Columbus Day, October 12, 1978, at 2307 hours. The other date read: October 12, 2191, 2307. The date that America was discovered and now the date I will discover the future.

"Holy Cow," I gasped.

I have not the meaning of your words. Please define? I heard Monroe ask.

Another confusing idiom for him. How to explain this one?

It is an expression of surprise, I said.

What is your surprise? He asked.

I just realized that today is my daughter's birthday.

BACK IN TIME

> *I got the globe, yeah, in the palm of my hand.*
> *Wherever I spin it, that's where I land.*—Pitbull

It is time to depart. Please take a seat and fasten your seat belt. It is still the law, Monroe said.

Yes siree Bob, I replied.

Who might Bob be? Monroe asked, confused by yet another idiom.

You know, that's a good question, Monroe. I have no idea who Bob might be. It's just another English expression, and I have no idea where it came from, I replied.

It occurred to me that it might be interesting to find out how some of these idioms originated, so I have added an appendix in the back of the book.

My blood pressure spiked as the female warrior approached, still smiling, and bent over to help strap me in.

"Hello," I said. " My name is…"

She quickly put one hand over my mouth and gestured with the other for me to be silent.

"Shhh. Names are forbidden," she whispered in my ear.

Her cleavage put a strain on my eyes and a bulge in my pants. When her hand brushed my leg, sparks flew from her fingertips and zapped me right between my legs.

"Whoa! Strap me in and fire up the flux capacitor Doc, cause here I come," I shouted, without thinking.

Monroe furrowed his brow, shook his head, and gave me another disgusting look. He must have thought I had a one-track mind and was a sex manic.

Hey kid, mine still works, so eat your heart out, I thought.

I probably should not have thought that, as I felt pressure building inside my head. It felt like he might be trying to fry my brain.

This type of communications was getting to be a pain in the neck, but I thought it might be best not to think it or I'd just might get myself fried. There had be a way to block some thoughts, I figured, but Monroe just wasn't wanting to tell me.

It occurred to me that I could just remove the helmet when I didn't want him hearing me, but then, that would probably freak him out. Can't have a freaked out grandson running around in a cramped up spaceship headed for the future.

Monroe pressed a large red button on the panel in front of him. I didn't recognize the symbol above it, but I swore I heard Star Trek Captain Picard say, *Engage.*

I thought Monroe might be playing with my mind. He looked me right in the eye and gave me a shit-eating grin.

Oh my God! Suddenly I observed something that I hadn't noticed before. Monroe had only three fingers and a thumb on each hand.

But before I could comprehend what I saw, I heard a loud hum and felt a sharp vibration. A tingling sensation covered my entire body and every hair stood straight up. In a blink of an eye, the date panels registered the same date. They both read October 12, 2191, 2307.

We're there already? I thought, as my body settled back to normal.

Of course, Grandpa. Time travels fast when you are having fun. If you do not know where you are going, you might end up someplace else! Monroe giggled.

Huh? Did I just hear an Aflac duck? Gee, the kid is starting to sound like Yogi Berra. At least he has developed a sense of humor, I thought.

Gotcha, Grandpa.

When we emerged from the mother ship, I felt a high, like two sheets to the wind. I had no idea time travel would provide such a buzz. But then, I had no idea I'd ever be going time traveling. I thought maybe I should do this more often.

Stepping out of the craft, I got a little woozy, like I might have had one too many rum and Cokes during the trip. It took me several minutes to get my feet on the ground. When I did, I noticed that we were in the same room at the base of the volcano. I looked up to see the same display of stars. It appeared we hadn't gone anywhere.

Son of a gun. How could that be? I wondered.

My doubts about this whole situation returned.

Was I being played for a fool?

This could have been the biggest elaborate practical joke ever played on a sucker like me. After all, it had been said that one was born every minute. This could be the joke that had the whole world laughing. So why was I crying? That Candid Camera had to be around there somewhere.

I am unfamiliar with Son of a gun, but you are no fool Grandpa, Monroe said. *Of course we are in the same room.*

Hey. Get off the grandpa kick. I'm only thirty-five. Let's just stick with Tom and Monroe, I thought.

As you wish, Tom.

I must have hurt his feelings cause he sounded hurt and had a sad look on his face.

We travel from time to time, not place to place. The ship stays in the same location, only in different time quantum's. Transport technology has not yet been invented to travel from location to location, Monroe explained.

Duh! Stupid me. How was I to know that Scotty hadn't been born yet? I thought.

Who is Scotty?

You don't know Scotty of Star Trek?

Then I remembered. Star Trek was a Sci-Fi show. *Forget it, Monroe. I was just thinking out loud.*

He probably doesn't understand how I could think out loud either.

We may have been in the same room at the base of the volcano, but it now had a far more sophisticated and futuristic appearance. There was even a R2D2-Star Wars type robot device scooting around the room. "Beep beep."

We should be on our way. Your brother is waiting, Monroe said, as he led me to one of the smaller craft parked near the mother ship.

Waiting for what? I wondered.

The Kid was about to fall into a nightmare.

CHAPTER ELEVEN

THE DREAMS

REALITY

So don't fool yourself into believing what you see.
It's only illusions, a prodigy.—Big Dismal

"A dream is an answer to a question we haven't learned to ask," said Fox Mulder, of *The X-Files*.

I say, "Dreams can be blocked memories buried in the subconscious."

In many ancient societies, dreaming was considered a form of supernatural communication, a means to predict the future, or a warning of something about to happen.

It is widely believed that dreams are the mind's way of sorting through our waking thoughts. Dreams are another reality with which we can interact. Dreams provide a signpost and a different perspective on our lives. They are offered to us nightly, free of charge, until they turn into nightmares, and then there is a price to pay.

Ever dream of another you? I had, and still do. In fact, I had dreamed of him for the past thirty-five years. He was a rambunctious rascal and could do the strangest things. He never seemed to age and had many women chasing after him. In fact, he reminded me a lot of myself.

So, why was I having these dreams? Did they transpire as a means of a mental connection (ESP) to another, like some twins are known to have? And just who in the hell was this other in my dreams? Was he really me, living a double or parallel life? So many questions to be answered. It was a complicated relationship.

This chapter might be a bit confusing, as dreams tend to be. Dreams occur within a matter of seconds but seem to last the whole night. They transpire in sleep, when the subconscious is the most relaxed. Most dreams fade from memory in a short time. For that reason, I would often arise as soon as I awoke from a dream and write it down. My wife, being a light sleeper, would usually wake and ask if I was okay.

"It's just a cramp, dear," I would tell her, or, "It's just gas, dear. Go back to sleep."

Here are some of dreams that I have had and recorded:

> *She says she wants to take our relationship to the next level and states she is three months with another's child. I wake up, somewhat confused.*

> *I reach in my mouth and pull on my upper front teeth. Out comes a skeleton mold of the inside of my face. I wake up, screaming.*

> *All my teeth begin to fall out. The same with the screws, springs, and plates that held them in place. I collect everything in a jar to give to the dentist, only I can't find him. I wake, grinding my teeth.*

I'm looking in the mirror and see a weird spectacle. Staring back at me is something half human and half alien. But I can recognize myself. I wake up, soaking in my sweat.

I sit at work to have lunch, open my lunch box, and grab a sandwich. It stinks, so I spread the bread apart. Squiggly worm-like critters spill out all over me. As they hit the air, they grow larger, saturating my entire body, and I can't breathe. I wake up, suffocating.

I'm soaring through the clouds like an eagle. I glimpse a huge shadow as something swoops down and attacks from above. It hits me with a tremendous force and I lose flight. I'm falling to the ground. I wake up, with my heart pounding.

Someone calls out to me. "Tom, help me. Where are you?" I wake up, talking to myself.

The female warriors are complete opposites. One has a pale blue complexion, with darker blue freckles. She has fiery red eyes, short curly flaming red hair, and plush rosy lips. Another has olive skin, with sparkly yellow eyes, and long straight blonde hair flowing over luscious watermelon breasts. The third is completely hairless, with black skin as dark as night and as smooth as silk. Her bedroom eyes change colors with each blink. Her three breast nipples point straight at me, enticing me to play with them. All three are exotic and naked. They absorb my body like a sponge. I wake up, hard as a rock.

I started a joke, which had the whole world crying. I wake up, laughing.

Three thugs have pinned me to the ground. I know with my martial arts training I can topple all three in a New York minute. So why am I letting them break my leg? I wake up, kicking.

I was on a field trip. An Asian princess sat behind me on the bus. Her inviting smile, hypnotic beauty, and sexy dark bedroom eyes are tantalizing. Departing the bus, she motioned to follow her home. Her sexy red thong was left on the front door knob, and the door was left ajar, an invitation to follow her trail. Articles of clothing left a path to her bedroom. I felt a tremendous surge of emotion and passion flowing through my veins as I entered the bedroom. Passion soon smothered my existence. I wake up, totally in love.

Some of the dreams were very peculiar and made no sense whatsoever. Others were exotic with imaginations, or were they fantasies, soon to be realities?

Did these dreams have something in common with my story? You would think so.

CHAPTER TWELVE

THE SUPPLEMENTARY

WHAT A WONDERFUL WORLD

I see trees of green, red roses too. I see them bloom, for me and for you. And I think to myself, what a wonderful world—Louis Armstrong

Monroe escorted me to a smaller craft, parked outside the mother ship. It had only two seats. It was a much smaller version of the mother ship.

I waved to the sexy female warrior, hoping that with a bit of luck, under different circumstances, and in time, we would cross paths again. I could tell by her smile and the twinkle in her eye that she had the same thoughts.

The smaller craft had a date panel similar to the one on the mother ship, only on a smaller scale. According to Monroe, the smaller craft could also zip in and out of time quantum's. When observed, that might explain why UFOs sometimes appeared to be in one place one minute and then suddenly accelerate and disappear the next. That might also explain why they were usually invisible to radar. Monroe never hinted as to why they had to fly in a formation of three.

With Monroe at the controls, our craft rose through the top of the volcano and headed to our destination. The cockpit window provided a 360 degree range of vision. I could make out two other craft similar to ours, tagging along. Before long, we could observe the sun rising, as we approached a huge transparent dome that shielded an entire city.

Monroe told me that there were only seven such cities on the planet, each on a separate continent, and each under a similar dome. The one we were approaching was located in the central part of what used to be called the United States of America. We were to land right smack dab in the heart of Kansas.

Each Dome had a population of approximately one million citizens. There was only one government, one language, one race, and one creed on the planet. Everyone sang the same song. Imagine that. Maybe there was hope for mankind after all.

Outside the dome, I observed a barren wasteland. According to Monroe, it was the result of pollution and one too many wars, before mankind got their act together. The Dome's were built because Earth's air had become sparse due to the lack of vegetation.

The Dome appeared to be approximately a hundred miles in diameter. Inside the dome I saw a Garden of Eden paradise, with greenery flourishing everywhere. Fountains and waterfalls galore were spouting sparkling colored water into the air. The streets sparkled with gold. There was no litter in sight.

I saw small automotive-type vehicles scooting around. They had no visible wheels, as they were suspended in the air about a foot above the ground. I thought it strange how man had invented the greatest invention of all—the wheel—and then had no use for it in the future.

I saw structures of different sizes and shapes that were impossible to describe. All I can say is that the city looked to be something you would see on some planet in a galaxy far far away. I had to remind myself I was still on Earth.

As we approached the dome, an entryway materialized. Just as we were about to enter, I heard a loud thump and felt a violent jerk.. The craft vibrated and suddenly pitched downward, slamming my head into the flight console in front of me. Warning sirens blared within the craft as it spun out of control. It was losing altitude fast. My chair began to spin out of control like riding a roller coaster. This immediately brought to mind one of my dreams. Only I knew this was no dream.

I heard a blood curdling scream coming from deep within my throat as I blacked out.

When I awoke I saw myself. I seemed to be outside my body looking in. I had on different clothes and was looking rather ragged. I was in need of a shave and a haircut. It looked like I had been put through the ringer. It didn't help that it felt like someone was pounding on my head with a hammer.

There were others gathered around. Humanoids of diverse colors, sizes, and shapes that I had never seen before. I thought that I had to be having another one of those dreams. Nothing seemed real.

Where am I? I thought. *Who are you guys?*

No one answered. I then realized that none of them were wearing a helmet. I felt my head and noted that mine was gone too.

"We removed your helmet. You won't be needing it anymore. They can't hear you now," myself said to me in a loud and clear voice.

"We also removed the tracking device from your toe. They can't track you now. Before you start freaking out, I'm Tom-Tom, your cloned brother." myself said to me.

I recalled I had suffered a blow on the head in the crash, so I figured I had to be hallucinating.

Did this guy just say he was my cloned brother?

Yeah, okay. Monroe told me about you. I just need to figure out if this is a dream or reality, I thought.

He didn't respond to my thought, so I said out loud,

"This can't be real. I got to dreamin'."

"Perhaps feeling is believing," Tom-Tom said, as he slapped me upside the head.

"Feel that? Think you're still dreaming now," he added.

That snapped me back to reality. It also pissed me off, and I jumped up, ready to fight back.

Everyone present jerked to attention and took a defensive position.

I quickly calmed down when I realized I was outnumbered.

"So what the hell is going on?" I asked.

"I sensed you were in the aircraft with the alien, so we shot it down and rescued you," Tom-Tom said.

"In an aircraft with an alien? Rescued me? I'm confused. I wasn't with an alien and I didn't need rescuing. What the hell are you talking about? I was coming to rescue you," I said.

"Rescue me? I don't need rescuing. Brother, you have been deceived," said Tom-Tom.

"Deceived? What are you talking about?"

To make a long story short, my cloned brother revealed a completely different history of mankind than what I had been led to believe by the alien called Monroe.

According to my brother, the abductors were in no way, kinfolk.

"How in the world can aliens be our kinfolk?" He asked with a chuckle.

He and the others had a hardy laugh, knowing I had fallen for a tall one. Come to find out, the abductors were not mankind's future generation, as Monroe had led me to believe. They were actually aliens from another world. It seemed I had been misled, and had fallen for his story hook, line, and sinker.

How embarrassing. How could I have been so gullible?

Bet you're thinking the same thing, huh?

According to my 'brother', the aliens had attacked and destroyed much of planet Earth twenty years earlier. Humans had put up a good fight, but were no match for a superior being. The Earth was scorched during the battle and made a wasteland. The aliens built the dome cities and enslaved most of the humans that survived.

Because of pollution and disease, plus the alien atmosphere inside the domes, their human slaves soon lost the ability to reproduce. The aliens ran low on slaves to handle their dirty work, so they would travel back in time to collect human sperm. Whatever it was they had in mind didn't work.

They then tried assimilating with humans. That didn't work the way they planned. They then decided to clone, but the clones were found to be sterile. They were fit to be tied.

Apparently the aliens hadn't read up on human history. Man always had and always will rebel against slavery. Clones were no exception. They, after all, were human too. Up until just a few months before, the humans and clones hadn't been much more than a thorn in the aliens' side. At least not until my clone, Tom-Tom, escaped the Dome.

He led a rebellion, and most of the clones, half-breeds, and humans escaped to the wastelands. They joined up with other surviving humans who were living in underground caves beneath the wastelands.

The aliens had to conjure up another plan. It involved traveling back in time to convince me to help them find Tom-Tom and put an end to the rebellion.

They tricked me into helping them find my clone, the rebel leader. They knew clones were on the same wavelength as their originals. We felt each other's presence, even through time warps. They figured I could lead them straight to him. Problem solved. They were right, too, but Tom-Tom foiled their plan and saved the day and maybe mankind, too, when he rescued me.

I know, you're probably thinking this is starting to sound like another one of those science fiction novels. Hey, I am just telling you like it is. No need to go rogue on me. I had no idea what I would be getting myself into when I decided to melt the memory blocks.

So here I was, suckered into believing in government conspiracies, UFOs, abductions, a sibling from the future, cloning, and now aliens. Not only that, I was now stuck in the future, right in the middle of a rebellion, in no man's land, with another major war on the horizon. The plot couldn't get much thicker.

Want 'a bet?

Move aside Buck Rogers, the Kid was about to come to the rescue, or discover he stepped in a bucket of shit and was stuck in the middle of some elaborate fairy tale. Question is, can he come out smelling like a rose?

CHAPTER THIRTEEN

THE BESIEGED

SOME NIGHTS

That's alright, I found a martyr in my bed tonight. She stops my bones from wondering just who I am, who I am, who I am, oh who am I, m-m-m.—Fun

At this point I began to wonder what had happened to Monroe, or whoever he was. It turns out that I was wearing my seatbelt, and apparently Monroe wasn't, because Tom-Tom told me he didn't think the alien survived the crash. They hadn't stuck around long enough to really found out. I found it ironic that Monroe had saved me from harm in my car crash and now couldn't save himself.

Okay. So what's next, I wondered.

It seemed I didn't have much of a choice. This would be a chance to be a real hero and save mankind, along with myself. If I didn't want to completely disappear from the map in my time quantum, I needed to step up to the plate in this one. I also needed to figure out a way to get back to the past. The only logical alternative to accomplish this would be to get back into one of the alien time craft. Unfortunately, though, at this point I was stuck out here in lord knows where, with no wheels in sight.

Not to worry, my brother said. He had a plan. A plan to destroy the dome and the aliens. A plan to save mankind in the past and the future. And a plan to return me to my time quantum.

He told me that we would accomplish all this with almost no weapons, a small group of clones, a few sick humans, and some half-human/half-aliens. Needless to say, I had a few second thoughts.

I reminded myself that Tom-Tom worked and lived inside the dome. He probably knew its Achilles' heel. I really had no choice but to provide a helping hand. How could I refuse? After all, I was expecting the adventure of all adventures.

"Let's go get 'em," I said.

"Okay, Brother, here's how it's going to go down," Tom-Tom replied.

His plan was a dilly. Indiana Jones would have been impressed.

"We depart at first light. You will be needing company to keep you warm tonight," Tom-Tom said.

"Company? To keep me warm? Sure, why not," I said, wondering what he might be implying.

The war with the aliens had drastically reduced the ratio of males to females. Females now outnumbered males seven to one. Those odds forced a change in social behavior. It became necessary for each male to accommodate more than one female. No matter how civilized humans became, when it came to sex, our instincts prevailed. We are the only species on Earth that uses sex for pleasure as well as reproduction. The night before battle was for pleasure.

Three attractive female warriors, of exotic nature, lay with me that night. Some of the genetically enhanced warriors had defected to the rebel side. They were extremely provocative and attractive in their own unique way.

One looked familiar. She was tall and had a pale blue complexion, with dark blue freckles covering her entire body. Her fiery red eyes pierced my soul. Her short curly flaming red hair and plush rosy lips set my body on fire. I recognized her from the mother ship. I could see by the twinkle in her eye and the smile on her face that she had been anticipating this moment.

Another was of medium height and had olive skin. She had sparkly yellow eyes with pupils that showed lighted candle wicks blowing in the wind. Her long straight blonde hair flowed over luscious watermelon breasts.

The third female was only about four feet tall, with skin as black as night and as smooth as silk. She was completely hairless from head to toe. She had bright shining electric bedroom eyes that changed colors each time she blinked. Her breasts were proud and pointed, with long protruding cherry red nipples that enticed me to play with them.

It got extremely warm in the cave that evening. In my time, this would have been many a man's dream, to bed three women at once. In a jiffy we were naked as jaybirds. Our lovemaking was fast and furious, turning into an all-night marathon. The more I gave, the more they wanted. Together the three absorbed my body like a sponge. We got so tangled that someone watching would not have been able to tell who was who. Our mating ritual must have resembled and sounded like wild cats in heat in a big city alley. Needless to say, this tomcat had one rousing, rollicking, and bruising night.

Sorry, I know I got you all worked up, but it's that dad gum PG-13 rating again. I can't elaborate anymore. You'll just have to use your imagination.

As you can imagine, I didn't get much sleep that night. The next morning I could hardly move, let alone go into battle with aliens. My brother had foreseen my predicament and had prepared a special energy drink. Good old Red Bull was still in production. In a New York minute, I was raring to take on anyone or anything.

Careful what you wish for, Tom, because you just might get it.

Tom-Tom assembled our small ragtag rebel force, which consisted entirely of misfits and unsung heroes, to make the journey through an underground tunnel, which led to the base of the alien dome.

We had to crawl on our hands and knees through slimy, rotten, smelly water. Where was that mask when I most needed it? This was not how I had envisioned a hero would travel. I darned near got bitten by a rat, more than once. Go figure, nearly two hundred years in the future and there were still rats! I hated rats!

Not only that, there were cock roaches everywhere. Crawling up my pant legs, shirt, and even getting into my hair. This was not what I had signed up for. If there hadn't been someone behind me, I'd have turned around and gone back to bed.

After crawling for what seemed an eternity, we finally reached our destination. You can imagine what we looked and smelled like. The aliens didn't have a chance. Our smell alone would have them on the run.

Somehow my brother knew how to penetrate the dome without setting off any alarms. Or so he thought. He must have had a connection on the inside, because just as we arrived, a small opening appeared in the dome.

"Move quickly, before it closes," he whispered.

There were about ten of us who scampered through the opening. Only nine made it. The tenth wasn't quick enough, and I heard a hiss and turned to see a lightening spark vaporize him as the opening closed on him. Ouch! That had to hurt. Thank God I wasn't last in line.

"We've got to keep moving," Tom-Tom said.

As bad as we stunk, I smelled that smell again from the cavern on Easter Island. Similar to the west wind that blows from Kansas. It was the atmosphere that the aliens breathed. It made me wonder if Jayhawks weren't aliens too.

Tom-Tom said that the air wasn't harmful to humans. It just stunk and made a person want to puke. But now was not the time to be throwing up.

"Just breathe slowly and keep moving," he advised.

The dome was actually a shield. Tom-Tom knew it had a power grid to keep it in place. That was our target. If we could disrupt the power source, the shield would collapse, leaving the aliens exposed to earth's atmosphere. Supposedly, they could survive by breathing our air, but it made them sick when they were exposed to it for a long period of time.

Our plan was to disable the power grid, capture or kill the aliens, steal a time craft, and whiz me back to 1978, where I could continue my dull life. Unfortunately, however, not all plans go according to plan, especially when dealing with a superior race that has just conquered you.

I'M HURTIN'

> Seems to me, my destiny is to be just hurtin',
> yeah hurtin'.—Roy Orbison

No sooner had we assembled inside the dome, we saw that we were surrounded. I about crapped my pants when I saw Monroe and several of his warriors pointing laser guns at us. It looked like he had survived the crash after all.

One of the warriors had my discarded helmet and forced it back upon my head.

We have been expecting you, Tom. Thank you for bringing your brother along, Monroe said.

Oh man. We fell right into their trap. The aliens must have planted a rat in our midst that had spilled the beans on us.

"You wouldn't happen to have a plan 'B' up your sleeve, would you?" I asked Tom-Tom.

He frowned and shook his head, "afraid not."

It looked like Monroe would be the hero this day. This wasn't going to look good on my resume.

Put them through the distillery, they smell like human waste. Then escort them to the prison compound, Monroe told his warriors.

After being stripped naked and sprayed with a fine sweet smelling mist, we were clothed in a gray metallic cloth outfit that everyone wore in this future culture. We were then marched to a building that resembled a prison compound and separated. I was put in a small room and strapped to what appeared to be a hospital operating bed, resembling those in our present-day hospitals. I was then left along to ponder my demise.

As I surveyed the room, I noticed a small table with a tray containing utensils. The utensils looked similar to what you see in a dentist's office.

This didn't look good. In fact, it became downright depressing. I was definitely between a rock and a hard place, and up the creek without a paddle. I couldn't remember having scheduled a dentist appointment for today.

Okay Tom, time to think this through. What would 007 do in a situation like this?

How about nudging the bed closer to the table, grabbing a sharp utensil knife in one hand, cutting through the strap, freeing myself from the bed, rescuing my comrades, escaping from the building, blowing up the shield's power grid, killing all the aliens, stealing a time craft, returning to 1978, and living happily ever after with my leading lady?

Absolutely brilliant idea, Tom!

There was only one small problem. This was not the movies and I was no James Bond.

Monroe brought me back to reality when he entered the room.

Well, earthling, there is no need for any more tricks, he said.

As you humans would say, it is time to get down to the nitty gritty, so I will get right to the point.

Thank you for leading us to your clone. We allowed the rebels to shoot down our craft and rescue you. We suspected they would plan to disable the shield, so we were waiting. Now you can provide us with the rebels' base location and their identities.

Apparently, their rat was the one who got vaporized, since Monroe still needed that information.

Uh oh. I was in a heap of trouble now. I hadn't bothered to get any names, except for Tom-Tom, and they already knew him. Plus, I don't recall Tom-Tom having GPS.

I would if I could. No one told me their name and I have no idea where their camp is, I said, knowing that was probably the wrong answer.

You can read my mind, so you must know I am telling you the truth, I thought.

Ah, but the rebels have probably trained you on how to hide some of your thoughts, said the alien.

I knew it! I suspected all along there was a way to hide them, and he had kept it from me.

I was hopeful you would cooperate. If not, then I will be forced to cause you much pain, Monroe said.

I'm telling you the truth. My mother taught me to never lie, I wisecracked.

By the look on his face, I could tell he wasn't appreciating my sense of humor. Somebody must have gotten up on the wrong side of the bed.

You will not think it to be funny when I demonstrate how much pain you can tolerate.

Monroe, or whatever his name was, picked up one of the utensils and started yanking out my teeth.

YOU SON-OF-A-BITCH, I screamed, as I spat blood at him.

That hurts. Don't you have some truth serum you could use?

I prefer primitive methods. Much more effective, the alien said, with that shit-eating grin on his face.

And, when I am done pulling out all your teeth, I will start on your fingernails and work my way to your toenails.

Christ! Who was it that outlawed water boarding? I had a bone to pick with them, right about then. It's time to abandon this adventurous hero stuff.

So what happened to 'when the going gets tough, the tough get going"?

Get real.

I told you I don't know any names or where they are hiding, I said, as I started to choke on the blood filling my mouth.

Oh, by the way, you wouldn't happen to have any Ibuprofen or Extra Strength Tylenol handy, would you?

I figured it couldn't hurt anymore to ask.

He must not have had a funny bone anywhere in that alien body, as he grabbed another tooth and yanked it out.

"YOU MOTHER FUCKER!" I shouted. (Mom, cover your ears).

Pardon my French. My temper was getting the best of me. I've heard that stressful situations can bring out the worst in people. I was definitely a little stressed at that moment. I would certainly be experiencing some post-traumatic stress disorder after this ordeal.

"That's the last straw," I said, as I spat more blood at the alien.

"Do you have any idea what my dentist will do to you when he sees what you've done. Then after he is done with you, I'm going to pluck those big weird eyes out and tear your mother fuckin' weird-looking head off that scrawny body of yours," I screamed at him.

Superman and Batman would have been proud, but I had to remind myself that this was not the comic books. That was real blood oozing out of my mouth and real pain shooting through my brain.

You are not in any position to make any threats, earthling, Monroe pointed out, as he yanked out the last remaining tooth.

It just so happened to be my only gold one. Can you imagine the price of gold in 2191? That little sucker would have done wonders for that cranky portfolio of mine.

I suppose you really do not know anything, or else you would have at least thought it by now, Monroe finally said. He turned and pressed a button on the wall.

Two other aliens entered the room.

Terminate him along with the others. They are of no use to us anymore, Monroe told them.

"HEY! WAIT! DAMN YOU TO HELL," I screamed at him.

"I still got fingernails and toenails?" I yelled, grasping at a last straw. Anything to delay my execution.

This wasn't how it was supposed to end. I thought I was the good guy. Good guys were supposed to prevail. Someone had gotten the script wrong.

The aliens weren't listening as they rolled me out into the hallway. I heard screams coming from behind each door we passed. They rolled me into a room that smelled of death and had me gagging even more. It was smoking hot from the inferno coming from a furnace.

Human and other types of corpses covered the floor. Squiggly worm-like critters crawled from their eye sockets, ears, noses, and mouths. They got bigger and bigger as I looked upon the frightful sight. Another dream had come true. Only now my dreams were turning into one humongous nightmare.

Time to wake up, Tom.

Problem was, I was already awake.

I had to admit that I was scared shitless. I'd never been this scared in my life. Fear within itself is impossible to define. It must be experienced to know its meaning. Right about now, its meaning was coming in loud and clear.

I had found out that this Buck Rodgers crap wasn't any fun after all. No wonder he had retired a long time before. It also seemed highly unlikely that my superheroes would come to my rescue anytime soon. It appeared I had met my Waterloo and would be disappearing from the face of the earth in the past, present, and future.

One of the aliens pulled out his laser gun, pointed it at my head, and said, *sweet dreams, earthling*, as he pulled the trigger.

"NO!" I screamed, as my head exploded, revealing the alien half of me. I heard the fat lady sing as I kicked the bucket and bit the dust. I was as dead as a door nail.

How can the Kid come back from the dead? Surely this isn't The End?

CHAPTER FOURTEEN

THE RECONCILIATION

"I think he is regaining conscious," my nightmare said.

Tom, can you hear me now? I recognized Monroe's thoughts. He must be trying to reach me on a cell phone.

Yes, I can hear you. What happened? Where am I?

My head felt like someone was pounding on it with a hammer.

You are in the infirmary, recovering from the crash.

Infirmary? Crash? Oh! My! God! My teeth! I gasped, as I remembered what had presumably happened.

I put my hand to my mouth and relaxed when I felt that my teeth were still there.

You have suffered a concussion in the accident and have been unconscious for two days, said Monroe.

An accident? What accident?

Our craft malfunctioned as we were entering the dome and we crashed. We were smart to be wearing our seatbelts.

But I saw you shoot me, I replied, confused.

Why would I shoot you?

You mean I'm not dead and you're not an alien?

An alien? No, Tom, you are not dead. Why on earth would you think me to be an alien? I have already explained all this? You must have had a hallucination in your coma.

A hallucination? In a coma? You got to be kidding me? You mean to tell me the whole last chapter was a hallucination? You certainly had me fooled. Wow, what a relief. Some hallucination, I thought.

Ha, another curve ball or was it a change-up. Bet you weren't expecting me to throw those pitches, were you? Hallucinations, nightmares and dreams. Are we getting a wee bit confused? I bet you thought for sure I was history. I know I did.

My headache quickly passed, and the futuristic healthcare had me back on my feet before you could shake a stick.

Ok. It's time to quit jacking around and find out why my future ancestors had cloned and brought me back to the future. We seemed to have gotten sidetracked somewhere. Hadn't Monroe said something about my cloned brother requiring my assistance?

Monroe and I left the infirmary and walked to another structure. Once inside, these futuristic facilities became translucent. You couldn't see any walls that separate the rooms.

In the lobby, you will never guess who I saw. As we entered, there, walking in the opposite direction, were my two no-name NASA buddies coming out. They were now wearing helmets too. Remember them? They were now wearing the same one piece gray metallic cloth outfit that everyone wore (except the warriors) in this time frame. One need not worry about being in style in this day and age.

I wondered what they were doing here in the future? I had thought I had left them in the past.

"Hey guys! What's up?"

Neither bothered to acknowledge my presence. I know they heard and saw me. Oh well, they had always been a little snobbish anyway.

Who needed snobbish friends? Then it dawned on me. They must have been cloned too. Were they here for the same reason as I?

As we passed through the lobby, an opaque image in 3-D could be seen in the middle of the room. It was suspended in midair and looked to be similar to a hologram. A crowd had gathered and was cheering the announcement that the Metropolis Cardinals (formerly St. Louis) had just come from four runs behind, in the bottom of the ninth inning, to win the 2191 World Series. Someone named Freese V had hit a grand slam!

Hey, Monroe, that's my favorite team. Go Cardinals! I said.

The announcer went on to say that this was their forty-third World Series championship, putting them one up on the Metropolis Yankees.

Seven of these championships had occurred during my lifetime. Well, I guess it was eight now.

1943 The year of my birth
1944 My first birthday
1964 USS *Hancock* entered the Vietnam War
1967 My first child was born (on the exact day).
1982 I became a born-again Christian.
2006 I retired
2011 I published my memoirs
2191 I met my cloned brother

As it turned out, Monroe was a Cubs fan, so he didn't share my enthusiasm. It also turned out that the poor Cubbies were still seeking their first World Series. Unbelievably! Hey, it was 2191 and they still hadn't won a World Series? It was hard to understand those Cubs fans, they had to be an unusual and complicated species. Still, you had to admire them for hanging in there all those years. I would imagine their tears over the years would form a pretty big lake.

As I surveyed the room, I noticed pictograms displayed. They would adjust in height to the person observing them. I walked over to them, noticed that they were commemoratives of human history that involved time travel.

The first one that caught my eye read:

"June 13, 1947. Roswell, New Mexico. In memory of three brave pioneer's who died in the first attempt to conqueror time travel."

Holy Cow! I thought. The Roswell story was true after all, except they mistook the bodies to be aliens.

Also on display were numerous old style military uniforms that covered many decades of history. A plaque displayed under one uniform caught my eye. It read:

"In memory of USN Grumman TBF-1 Avenger Torpedo crewmen. Flight 19, Dec. 5, 1945. Bermuda Triangle."

I remember reading about them, I told Monroe, as he joined me.

It is one of the greatest mysteries of human history.

In the early days of time travel and abductions, unfortunately, some things went wrong, Monroe replied.

I sensed he didn't want to continue the conversation.

Not to change the subject, but how about a round of golf? They do still play golf, don't they? I asked.

Yes, we do, but at the present we have more important matters to attend to, he said, as he guided me toward the elevators.

What could be more important than golf? I thought, knowing full well he could hear me, as I saw him roll his big eyes.

I bet you're afraid I'd whoop your ass.

That stopped him dead in his tracks. His glare and then his thought went far beyond my comprehension.

Okay, forget it, I said. *No need to get all riled up. I'm just messing with you.*

We took an elevator to the fifth floor. I guess you would call it an elevator. It was nothing like I'd ever ridden and nothing I could possibly describe. It was like riding on air. There were no visible walls or floors. It messed with my equilibrium and I kept losing my balance. Monroe had to help steady me. It was kind of scary because I kept feeling like I would fall through to the ground floor.

We departed the elevator and walked down a hallway. The hallway floor was also translucent, and I could see through all the way down to the bottom floor. Again, my equilibrium was thrown off. It was the weirdest sensation!

We finally settled in a plain small room. Once in the room, the walls, floor and ceiling became opaque, rather than translucent. The room contained only a chair and a couch, with a small, low table wedged between them. A man who looked to be my twin jumped up from the chair to greet me as we entered.

"Hello, brother. I am so excited to meet you," Tom-Tom said as he grabbed and shook my hand.

It reminded me of when my half-brother Mike had greeted me for the first time in the hallway in junior high, except for the fact that there had been no handshake then.

It was weird to be looking at myself and yet not using a mirror. I suppose identical twins would know the feeling. Tom-Tom's handshake was firm, so I knew he was no hologram.

He wasn't wearing a helmet, so I spoke out loud, "Hi, nice to meet you too."

It was all I could think to say, as the cat seemed to have my tongue. It's not every day one meet's oneself.

D-Day had arrived. To say I was nervous and a little apprehensive would have been an understatement. The air became thick with suspense. You could have heard a pin drop, as I waited for Monroe to explain exactly what I was doing here.

We require the two of you to trade places, was the bombshell he dropped.

Tom, we need you to stay here in this time frame and have Tom-Tom take your place in your time frame, my grandson continued.

Trade places? You want me to trade places with my clone? I asked, as I could scarily believe what I was hearing.

That is why he was created, Monroe added.

Monroe reminded me that human gene splicing and evolution had caused future human generations to become sterile. Humans could no longer reproduce. Cloning was supposed to have solved the problem. Unfortunately, the clones were sterile too. A plan was adopted to have the clones trade places with their originals. The originals would come and stay in the future in order to help preserve the human race. *Are you getting this?*

That's what all this had been about from the very beginning? Starting with my abduction outside Clinton, to the abductions in Oklahoma and California. Stealing my sperm, enhancing my genes, cloning me, and all because the future human generation went sterile and couldn't reproduce.

I can hear you saying it now, *who is going to believe this shit?*

Monroe further explained that abductees couldn't just disappear from their time quantum. It would disrupt future events and cause a tear in the time warp. That's where the clones came in. The clones would continue with their human original's life events and life span. This would keep the time line from erupting.

The originals selected for this switch were those known to have had no more children and to have lived a normal life span. This switch would not affect history or timelines. No one would suspect it had occurred, not even the clones, as they would be given a memory block.

Many clones and originals had already agreed to the switch and were in their places. My clone was ready and willing to take my place. He was anxiously awaiting my decision.

Wow! I think I will need a few minutes to absorb all this, let alone believe it, I said.

I understand, but you need to make a decision within the hour, Monroe said.

"What's the hurry? You should have all the time in the world."

It is too complicated for you to comprehend the vast details. Press this button on the wall when you have made your decision, he replied.

With that, he and Tom-Tom departed, leaving me to contemplate the situation. Do I really have a choice? What would they do if I refused?

Actually, I had already made up my mind. There was no way I could be dreaming all this up. I had finally become a bona fide believer.

This led me to wonder about something else that I had had in the back of my mind. With all this time travel and technology, maybe Monroe could do me a little favor, in return for me helping save mankind from extinction. He hadn't been gone for more than a few minutes when I pushed the button.

I would like a favor in return, I told him, when he returned.

What favor would that be? He asked.

Can you find out what happened to my second wife, Fiza? She disappeared a couple months ago.

I had no idea if he could achieve such a feat, but I was compelled to ask, considering all of the advanced technology he had at his disposal.

Give me her full name, date of birth, and the date, location, and approximate time she disappeared, he said.

I provided him the information.

I will return in a few minutes, he said.

That had to be the longest few minutes of my life.

Do I really want to know? I kept asking myself.

I am sorry to have sad news for you. Are you sure you want this information, Monroe said, upon his return.

Yes, I need to know.

She was taken back to Saudi Arabia by her brothers and put into a Bedouin tribe.

I had suspected that.

She was sold into slavery and used to entertain visiting male tribe members. She committed suicide two weeks ago, (in your time frame) through the bite of a king cobra. Suicide was the only escape that would keep you and your children safe. I am so sorry, Tom. She basically sacrificed her life for your sake.

A river of emotions flowed through my heart and soul. I started bawling like a baby.

Why can't you go back in time and abduct her just before she dies? I cried.

I am sorry, Tom, it does not work that way, Monroe replied. *Her disappearance would disrupt the time quantum.*

Maybe you could clone her and have the clone take her place, I pleaded.

We cannot ask a clone to take the place of someone who dies before their time. I am sorry, but you must face the fact that she is gone. If you wish, I can instill a memory block to erase her memory from your mind.

No, I said. *I want to remember her, always.*

I do not intend to rush you, but I must have your decision soon. Perhaps there is someone else you should talk to, Monroe said, as he reached to open the door.

She might help you make up your mind.

Was Monroe throwing another monkey wrench into the equation? Now who could this person possibly be?

The door opened and in walked—you'll never guess who? Golly! Surprise, surprise, surprise. Not even Gomer Pyle could have said it any better.

In walked Claudia, my first wife, the one who went rogue on me and started this whole shebang in the first place. I bet the look on my face would have stopped my granddaddy's clock.

I could perceive a major meltdown coming, with all the different emotions swarming through me. First I was shocked, and then came hurt, followed by anger, anxiety, and last but not least confusion.

You can have a few minutes alone to talk, Monroe said, as he departed the room.

"Hello Tom. I hope you now realize everything we went through wasn't my fault," were the first words out of Claudia's mouth.

"I had already made my decision a long time ago. My clone, CJ, replaced me right after our son was born. It was she who discovered how to melt her mind block and became confused and divorced you, not me."

"You don't say," was all I could muster.

The cat had my tongue again. Everything seemed to be happening in slow motion.

"Legally, we are still married, though in this society there are no marriages. Still, we can have a friends-with-benefits relationship and help preserve the human race. That is our primary purpose now, to reproduce. I am currently three months with child. What say you?"

"Whatever?"

What else was there to say?

This better not be another dream. I was about dreamed out.

It was going to take a while to comprehend all this. The human mind was limited in capacity and this one was getting stretched to the limit.

"I realize you must be shocked to see me," Claudia said.

"I have been there and know the feeling. But Monroe will need a decision soon," she reminded me.

Needless to say, by this point I was a little perplexed. My intellectual capacity had been maxed out. I felt like I was either in the *Twilight Zone* or in the *Outer Limits*. The picture was getting fuzzy and out of alignment.

Please standby. The Kid needed a quick adjustment.

CHAPTER FIFTEEN

THE SURROGATE

ROCKET MAN

And I think it's gonna be a long long time, till touchdown brings me round again to find I'm not the man they think I am at home. Oh no no no. I'm a rocket man.—Elton John

Well comrades, you should know Tom well enough by now to know his decision. He had a love for adventure and this would be the adventure of his lifetime! How could he have refused?

So, behold, it was I, Tom-Tom, Tom's clone, who got a memory block and was sent back to 1978 to continue his legacy.

So far as the world knows, the visit from NASA never happened. There might have been a new kid in town, but no one, including me, knew the difference. No one—not Tom's parents, his sisters, his brother Mike, his children, or his friends—had the slightest suspicion.

I am no different from Tom. All of his memories and experiences were programmed into me. We now share the same appearance, memories, personality, age, and health. We are more than twins; we are the same.

I would, however, spend the next several years gallivanting around, searching for an identity and a purpose. I became a restless spirit on an endless flight. I sought fame and fortune, seeking that heart of gold. It took several more relationships, two more marriages, and a few more heartbreaks, heartaches, and comebacks before I finally landed on solid ground.

CJ, after discovering she was a clone, had trouble accepting her reality. She eventually sent the children to live with me. Even though she suspected, she was not yet certain that I was also a clone.

The next few years were difficult, as I tried to adapt to being a parent. Learning parenthood right when your children turn into teenage monsters was demanding. There were a few times I just wanted to run away. Somehow, we all survived.

Then I finally met my heart of gold and the 'love of my life'. Her name was Karen. We fell in a sensible love. The way you fall asleep: slowly, but surely.

Now I am getting close to the final curtain. I have discovered that aging doesn't take a special ability or talent. No one ever gets to practice it; it just sneaks up on you. It's gotten hard to recognize the old fart who makes those funny faces and stares back at me in the mirror. Whatever happened to that perfect age when you're old enough to know better and too young to care? Gone, but not forgotten.

If you read my original memoirs, then you might have thought you knew my story. But you didn't, because I didn't, at the time. If you haven't read my original memoirs, you might find them interesting. The memory blocks kept me from seeing the hidden revelations. But, thanks to CJ, I eventually learned how to melt them and discovered my distinctiveness.

It took writing my memoirs before I suspected a thing. Once I took CJ's advice and was willing to fast and abstain from sex, a whole new world revealed itself. Never in my wildest dreams would I have suspected myself to be a clone. Our creators hadn't figured that we would learn to melt our memory blocks. CJ outwitted them.

We needn't be concerned that the abductors or the government may discover that some of us now know the truth. I would suspect they both already know. They aren't concerned because they know that everyone will just think us to be crazy UFO wackos. It could be that the definition of "wacko" will have to be redefined someday. But until then, at least there are a few of us who know the truth and know who we really are.

That being said, it raises another interesting question. Do clones have a soul? I do know right from wrong and have all human traits, but does that make me human? I suppose I won't know the answer to that question until I arrive at the pearly gate.

I have heard there could be as many as three million abductees in America. There is no telling how many more are spread around the globe. Of course not all have been cloned. But I don't know that for a fact.

I can identify at least one of you besides CJ, but I won't reveal who this is, as you have yet to discover it yourself. I warned you in the beginning that my story could change your life and that you might never be the same.

If you have the slightest inclination that you may have been abducted and cloned, then you now know how to find out for sure. Become a vegetarian, fast and abstain from sex for a while and see if you have any memory blocks that melt. It will take some courage to make the necessary sacrifice, but the results should answer your questions once and for all.

Only a few will be willing to put it on the line. I suspect there will be many who really don't want to know. I can't really blame you for wanting to stay tucked in your comfortable and secure little world. It will be interesting to find out who the brave ones will be.

So you now know, it is I, Tom-Tom who wrote both the original memoir and this revised edition. Tom has been absent from this timeline since 1978. I wouldn't worry about him, though. I have been having some pretty exotic dreams lately, and those dreams indicate that he is gallivanting around in the future, footloose and fancy-free, on a quest to save the human race from extinction. Tom is also helping the human race to revert back to our present-day appearance. Perhaps someday the abductors will not be mistaken for aliens anymore.

In the meantime, if you should someday happen to see a UFO, the least you could do is wave. After all, its occupants could be some of your *kinfolk*. ☺

EPILOGUE

I would bet many of you are probably thinking that my story is a bit far-fetched. You might want to keep in mind, that once upon a time, a man walking on the moon seemed a bit far-fetched.

You might be wondering if I have been smoking weed, lost my marbles, or maybe have a fertile imagination that went wild? Well, I haven't smoked weed for years. I suppose losing a few marbles and having a wild imagination could be debatable. Is my story a memoir or is it a sci-fi tale written in the style of a memoir? It could be a blend of reality (true life events) with my imagination. That said, I do wonder where and how the imaginations originated. Could they have been memories, blocked by unknown entities, that were buried deep into my subconscious? If this were to be true, wouldn't that make my imagination my reality?

Who is to say that the world we live in is our reality? Certainly not those of you who might have blocked memories but are unwilling to make the necessary sacrifice to discover who you really are. Hopefully, my story has offered some food for thought. But who among you is hungry? Those of you who may have tried Claudia's ascetic lifestyle, only to be left hungry and horny, will be the biggest doubters.

My intention all along was not to convince you one way or the other. It was to give you a story that would entertain, mystify, startle, and hopefully tickle your intuition.

As Albert Einstein wrote:

> *The most beautiful thing we can experience is the mysterious. It is the source of all true art and science. He to whom this emotion is a stranger, who can no longer pause to wonder and stand rapt in awe, is as good as dead; his eyes are closed and he is a stranger unto himself.*

LOL

Thank you for taking the time to read my story. I would appreciate if you would also take the time to write and post a review on Amazon: amzn.to/PwRRlc and/or my website: www.thomaslhay.com.

If you enjoyed this story you might want to read my original memoirs, *The Comeback Kid, The Memoirs of Thomas l. Hay.* It is available where books are sold.

IDIOMS

Idioms, to make a long story short, are actually nonsense, yet hit the nail on the head. We know what these phrases mean; we all use them. But where do these funny and nonsensical statements come from? Since when can you know the ropes, knock on wood or wag the dog?

An idiom generally is an expression different from its literal meaning. Often, only people in a particular region or class understand it. Some first appeared in the Bible or were penned by Shakespeare. Today, with the proliferation of mass media, they can spread thick and fast.

Those foreigners who learn the English language are surely scratching their heads. Most of the idiom's I used in this story confused Monroe as he tried to comprehend what it was I had said. If you're like me, you may have started to wonder just where they came from.

To help you understand, I composed a list of most of the idioms I used. You might find their meaning and origin interesting.

NOTE: Even with the Internet, it was impossible to learn the origins of some of these idioms. Some of the stories of origin that I did find are simply that: stories. Although the intricate stories can sound plausible, often a simple explanation is the real answer. That's how extraordinary and confusing the English language can be. So, on that note, let's:

GIVE IT A SHOT OR GIVE IT YOUR BEST SHOT

Meaning: To give it a try, to endeavor.

Origin: Unclear. It might have a military origin. The term "best shot" came from a sixteenth-century shooter who could hit enemies or targets most accurately. It became a common phase in the twentieth century.

STOP AND SMELL THE ROSES

Meaning: To pause. Take time to appreciate.

Origin: Most think it became popular after Ringo Starr's song in 1981.

SMACK DAB

Meaning: In essence, it means "slapped precisely in the center."

Origin: First used in 1892. Smack is a transitive verb meaning to strike sharply and with a loud noise. Dab is a chiefly British word meaning clever or skilled. Put the two together and you have an idiom.

CLOUD NINE

Meaning: A state of elation/happiness.

Origin: This term originated with the U.S. Weather Bureau in the 1950s, and denotes the fluffy cumulonimbus clouds that people find attractive. Why the number '9' is unclear.

BRAND SPANKING NEW

Meaning: A new or unused object.

Origin: From doctors spanking newborn babies to make them cry so that they will start breathing.

SPILL THE BEANS

Meaning: To divulge a secret, especially to do so inadvertently or maliciously.

Origin: There is the word "spill," meaning divulge, but why beans? It could have come from almost anything. One theory: The origin of this expression is sometimes said to be an ancient Greek voting system. The story goes that white beans indicated positive votes and black beans negative votes. Votes had to be unanimous, so if the collector "spilled the beans" before the vote was counted, the vote was halted.

WHAT IN SAM HILL

Meaning: This is a euphemism, an inoffensive expression used to substitute for terms or words that might offend.

Origin: Who is Sam Hill anyway? Some say he was a proponent of the Pacific Highway, the railroad built to reach the West in the 1800s. Those who knew him thought him to be crazy. Anyway, if he could have a nickel for every time someone has used his name, he would have a wealthy estate.

GRASPING AT STRAWS

Meaning: A desperate attempt.

Origin: This term comes from the fact that a drowning person will grab at anything, including a straw, to keep from drowning.

PUT A BUG IN YOUR EAR

Meaning: A reminder, a hint, or suggestion relating to a future event.

Origin: Presumably likens the buzzing of an insect to a hint, although the exact analogy is unclear.

BETWEEN A ROCK AND A HARD PLACE

Meaning: Stuck between two bad options.

Origin: In 1917, mine workers in Bisbee, Arizona were faced with a choice between harsh and underpaid work at the rock-face part of the mine or face unemployment and poverty. Darn if you do, and darn if you don't.

PULLING YOUR LEG

Meaning: Fooling about something. A joke being played.

Origin: No one seems to know. One speculation is that it might originated from the fact that during the old days in England when people were hung and left to swing in the wind, poor children would pull the hanged person by his or her leg in order to dislodge valuables from his or her pockets. Adults would tell the children to leave them alone and not to pull one's leg. Another theory has it that friends and relatives would often try to end the suffering of the hanged by pulling their legs in hopes of breaking their neck.

NEST EGG

Meaning: Savings set aside for later use.

Origin: The allusion is to putting a real or china egg onto a hen's nest to encourage the hen to lay. The connection between this and the idea of savings isn't exactly clear. It may be that the idea was that the egg that was put into the nest could be retrieved and used again after the hen had laid.

BITE OFF MORE THAN YOU CAN CHEW

Meaning: Taking on a task that is too great to complete.

Origin: Watching children stuff their mouths too full, causing difficulty in swallowing. Also slang referring to the use of plug tobacco.

THE WHOLE NINE YARDS

Meaning: The whole way or measure.

Origin: This is another one whose origin no one knows for sure. One theory is it had to do with eighteenth-century women's gloves that went up to their elbows. They wore them when attending an important event, such as a ball or tea at the palace. The gloves had nine buttons.

NITTY GRITTY

Meaning: The specific or practical details, getting to the heart of the matter.

Origin: The origin of this idiom is somewhat unpleasant and a little unexpected. If you can stomach it, read on. It seems to derive from nits (small lice) found in unclean pubic hair plus the tiny, gritty pieces of dried feces found in unwashed anal hair. In America, the term was popularized by black militants in the Civil Rights movement.

JOSHING

Meaning: Kidding, fooling someone.

Origin: If you think I'm a character, wait until you read about this guy. Josh Tatum was a deaf mute, but a very enterprising man. In 1883 the U.S. mint came out with a new nickel. It was deemed the Liberty Nickel and on the reverse side it had a large Roman numeral V stamped on it. Josh noticed this and the fact that it was nearly the same size as the U.S. $5 gold piece. With the help of a friend familiar with gold electroplating base metal, they turned these coins into a fortune.

Josh went from town to town, shopping in shops and stores. He was careful not to buy anything that cost more than a nickel, and then he would hand over one of the gold-plated nickels. The clerk, thinking it to be a $5 gold piece, would give him back $4.95 in change. He soon amassed a small fortune. The law eventually caught up with him but ironically he was found not guilty because he had purchased items that cost so little. Hence the saying, "You're not Joshing me, are you?"

LET THE CAT OUT OF THE BAG

Meaning: Give away a secret.

Origin: Alludes to the dishonest practice of a merchant substituting a worthless cat for a valuable pig, a fact that was discovered only when the buyer got home and opened the bag.

HOLD YOUR HORSES

Meaning: slow down, be patient.

Origin: This expression alludes to a driver making horses wait by holding the reins tightly, something that's not too common in modern society.

PIPE DOWN

Meaning: Stop talking, be silent. Hush. Turn the cell phone off.

Origin: The idiom is also used as an imperative. It comes from the navy, where signals for all hands to turn to and turn in were sometimes sounded on a whistle or pipe.

CLEAR AS A BELL

Meaning: To be understood clearly.

Origin: Bells, such as the ones used in churches, have a loud and clear sound, which can be heard for miles.

NUTS

Meaning: Strange, eccentric, crazy, or insane. Used also to express contempt, disappointment, or refusal. Could pertain to all of us old farts.

Origin: The word "nut" was used as a slang term for "head" around 1820. Gradually it acquired the meaning not merely of "head," but of "something wrong in the head." This one really got into Monroe's head.

HOLY COW

Meaning: An exclamation of surprise.

Origin: This term comes from the Indian belief that cows are sacred. I don't know what that has to do with being surprised. Unless it refers to waking up one morning and finding you are on Medicare.

TWO SHEETS TO THE WIND

Meaning: A state of extreme incapacity due to being tipsy, putting it nicely.

Origin: The phase is properly "three sheets to the wind." Americans always shorten everything. A sheet is the rope on a sailboat that holds the clew of a sail tight and under control. When three come unsecured, the boat becomes unsteady.

SON OF A GUN

Meaning: Used to express annoyance, disappointment, or surprise.

Origin: This one is a dilly. It generally refers to a person who is a rascal or scamp. My brother comes to mind, but then I am probably coming to his mind.

One nautical myth suggests that in order to keep sailors in the British Navy from deserting, they were kept onboard while in port. The captain would allow "wives" to come aboard. Cramped quarters caused the "wives" to sling hammocks between the cannons. The expression actually questions the legitimacy of those who were born after the encounters in these hammocks. Most must have been males, since you don't hear "daughter of a gun."

HOOK, LINE, AND SINKER

Meaning: Falling for a prank, or to be complete.

Origin: This idiom refers to a fishing pole. You have to have all three items on a pole to catch a fish. Wait a minute, don't you need bait too?

GOT UP ON THE WRONG SIDE OF THE BED

Meaning: Having a rough or horrible day.

Origin: This alludes to the ancient superstition that it was bad luck to put the left foot on the floor first when getting out of bed. By the 1800's the expression was associated more with ill humor than misfortune.

UP THE CREEK WITHOUT A PADDLE

Meaning: In trouble, in a serious predicament.

Origin: This idiom conjures up the image of a stranded canoeist. President Truman used the phrase in a 1918 letter and it caught on from there.

FIT TO BE TIED

Meaning: To be furious.

Origin: This refers to the practice of binding uncontrollable, dangerous people into straitjackets.

IT'S NOT OVER TILL THE FAT LADY SINGS

Meaning: Don't assume the outcome of some activity until it has actually finished.

Origin: This term comes from the opera in the eighteenth century, when many of the lead singers were large women and they would sing the finale.

KICK THE BUCKET

Meaning: You die…plain and simple.

Origin: This phase originates from the French. In slaughterhouses, the rail on which pigs are hung after slaughter to drain off the blood is known as the bucket bar. Muscle spasms after death sometimes lead to the dead pig twitching as if to kick the bucket bar.

BITE THE DUST

Meaning: Suffer defeat or death.

Origin: This term was popularized by American Western films in the 1930s, in which either cowboys or Indians were thrown from their horses to the dusty ground when shot.

YES SIREE BOB

Meaning: Yes, indeed. I will agree or accept.

Origin: This expression is used as a euphemism for God. The "siree" is a modification of "sir."

GALLIVANTING

Meaning: To roam about in search of pleasure or amusement, to flirt.

Origin: Perhaps an alternation of the word gallant. Sorry, that was all I could find.

FOOTLOOSE AND FANCY FREE

Meaning: Unattached romantically.

Origin: Another case of human conduct likened to the movements of a sail. On most sailing vessels the lower edge of the main sail, known as the foot, is lashed to a boom to keep it stretched and properly shaped, but there are exceptions. Some vessels have no boom and the sail is allowed to hang loose along the foot. Loose-footed sails, as they are called, are said to have a mind of their own and are difficult to control.

NEW YORK MINUTE

Meaning: Faster than normal.

Origin: The theory is that everything happens faster in New York City. We slow-walking, slow-talking country folk have to quicken our pace to keep up.

COCK AND BULL STORY

Meaning: Tall tale, unbelievable.

Origin: This phrase dates back to the eighteenth century, at the height of the great coaching era, when the town of Stony Stratford was an important stopping-off point for mail and passenger coaches travelling between London and the north.

Travelers on these coaches were regarded as a great source of current news from remote parts of the country, which would be imparted in the town's two main inns, The Cock and The Bull. The two establishments rapidly developed a rivalry as to which could furnish the most outlandish and scurrilous tales.

TICKLED PINK

Meaning: Delighted.

Origin: The tickling here isn't the light stroking of the skin—it's the figurative sense of the word that means "to give pleasure or gratify." The concept is of enjoyment great enough to make the recipient glow with pleasure.

SHIT

Meaning: Something stinks, it not quite right.

Origin: The most functional English word of all. As you know, I used it more than a few times and you hear it said it every day of your life. To prove that it is the most fundamental English word consider this:

You can smoke shit, buy shit, sell shit, lose shit, find shit, forget shit, and tell others to eat shit. There are lucky shits and dumb shits. There is horse shit and chicken shit.

You can throw shit, sling shit, catch shit, shoot shit, step in shit, shit a brick, and better duck when the shit hits the fan.

You can give a shit or find yourself in deep shit. Things can look like shit and there are times when you feel like shit.

You can have too much shit, not enough shit, the right shit, the wrong shit, or a lot of weird shit.

Sometimes everything you touch turns to shit and other times you fall into a bucket of shit. When all is said and done, shit happens. No way to escape shit. I bet by now you are thinking that all this is nothing but a bunch of bullshit.

Last, but not least. Now, as you know I have travelled to many places, most often in cahoots. Apparently, that is a place you can't go alone. You have to be in cahoots with someone.

I have been to incognito also, but I hear no one recognizes you there.

I would like to go to conclusions, but you have to jump to get there.

I have also been in doubt, but it's a sad place to visit.

One of my favorite places to be is in suspense. It can really get the adrenalin flowing.

SONG APPENDIX

Here are the song and event descriptions, listed in the order they appear:

SONG EVENT DISCRIPTION

Welcome to My World . . . . Introduction
Country Road . . . . Abduction
New Kid in Town. . . . . Baby chicks
Runaway . . . . Bad boy
The Way we Were. . . . . Memories
It's All in the Game . . . . Holy cow
Bad Moon Rising. . . . . Black sheep
Family Tradition . . . . Good ole days
Against All Odds . . . . .Stupid is
Reunited. . . . . Wicked witch
The Wayward Wind . . . . .He ain't heavy
Puppy Love . . . . .Heart throb
Slow Poke. . . . . Ugly duckling
Hanky-Panky. . . . . Little critters
Lipstick on Your Collar . . . . .Wipeout
For the Good Times . . . . Teen behavior
No Future in the Past. . . . . .Get out of Dodge
In the Navy . . . . .World traveler

Bend Me, Shape Me. . . . . .Boot camp
I Can See Clearly Now. . . . . Manhood
Western Union. . . . . Gifted
Beyond the Sea. . . . . .At home
South of the Border . . . . On the run
Like a Virgin . . . . The birds and bees
SOS. . . . . UFO
Why Do Fools Fall in Love. . . . . Gullible
Should I Stay or Should I Go . . . . Indecisions
Achy Breaky Heart . . . . Heartaches
Kansas City . . . . Lost relatives
Pretty Woman .Tied the knot
Heartbreak Hotel. . . . . Lost dream
The Wanderer .Westward ho
Arabian Nights. . . . . Land of enchantment
Macho Man. . . . . .Back in the saddle
On the Road Again . . . . .Mysteries
Poison Ivy. Forbidden fruit
All Night Long. . . . . Soul mate
Dream Lover . . . . Romance
Take it to the Limit. . . . . .Playing with fire
Oops, I Did it Again. . . . . Love on the run
It's Only Make Believe. . . . . False hopes
The End of the World . . . . .Lost soul mate
Time. . . . . Plan implemented
Do You Want to Know a Secret. . . . . . Plan revealed
Hello. . . . . .Hallucinations
Back in Time . . . . Saddle up
Reality . . . . Illusions
What a Wonderful World. . . . . .The future
Some Nights. . . . . Galaxy playboy
I'm Hurtin'. . . . . .Post-traumatic stress
Rocket Man . . . . Identity crises

AUTHOR AUTOBIOGRAPHY

Thomas L. Hay was raised in the Golden Valley of Clinton, Missouri. He is a graduate of the 1961 Clinton Senior High class. He retired after thirty-nine years with TWA/American Airlines. He enjoys fishing, golfing, writing, and singing Karaoke. He currently resides in Lake Waukomis, Missouri, with his lovely wife Karen, along with some hyperactive squirrels, too many irritating geese, and a few cranky old catfish.

EDITOR REVIEW

An Abduction Revelation is an excellent story and a gripping book. I couldn't wait to read what happened next, as the story picks up momentum with each page.

Kerry Genova, Writers Resource, Inc.

Printed in the United States
By Bookmasters